THE
WIZARD'S DOG
FETCHES
THE GRAIL

Also by Eric Kahn Gale

The Wizard's Dog

THE
WIZARD'S DOG
FETCHES
THE GRAIL

Eric Kahn Gale
illustrated by Dave Phillips

CROWN BOOKS
FOR YOUNG READERS
NEW YORK

Text copyright © 2018 by Eric Kahn Gale
Jacket art and interior illustrations copyright © 2018 by Dave Phillips

All rights reserved. Published in the United States
by Crown Books for Young Readers, an imprint
of Random House Children's Books,
a division of Penguin Random House LLC, New York.

Crown and the colophon are registered trademarks
of Penguin Random House LLC.

Visit us on the Web! rhcbooks.com

Educators and librarians, for a variety of teaching tools,
visit us at RHTeachersLibrarians.com

Library of Congress Cataloging-in-Publication Data is available upon request.
ISBN 978-0-553-53740-6 (trade) — ISBN 978-0-553-53742-0 (ebook)

Printed in the United States of America
10 9 8 7 6 5 4 3 2 1
First Edition

Random House Children's Books supports
the First Amendment and celebrates the right to read.

THE WIZARD'S DOG
FETCHES THE GRAIL

PART I

1

The Dog Who Would Be King

HE TOLD ME NOT TO SPEAK. MOST DOGS WOULD FIND THAT AN easy command to follow. But I'm not like most dogs. I'm a wizard's dog.

Still, Merlin was my master, and as my pack shivered together in the rain outside the tavern door, I closed my mouth and wagged my tail in assent.

"Thank you, Nosewise," Merlin said, pushing a wet strand of hair from his brow. Water pooled in the brim of his hat and streamed down his long white beard into his robes. He glanced at Arthur and Morgana. "And you two. Are we clear on what to share and what to hide?"

"We are," said my girl, Morgana, covering her eyes to keep them from the rain. She shivered in her tunic and elbowed Arthur in the ribs.

"Me too," said Arthur, my boy, patting the cloth pack bound tightly against his back. "I can keep a secret."

"Right, then. Let's not make a scene," Merlin said, and pushed open the heavy tavern door.

Warm yellow light filled the hall, and the air was scented with mead and meat. I felt my fur dry in the toasty air and my mouth water from the delectable smells. I turned to Morgana to say how nice it seemed, but then I remembered: *Don't speak.*

"Is this the best place to keep a secret?" she whispered to Merlin as the four of us shuffled into the tavern. The place was packed with rowdy guests eating and drinking their fill. Some warmed their damp feet by the fire, and others laughed uproariously over cards.

"It's the only tavern around," Merlin said. "Perhaps we'll go unnoticed here."

"Arthur? Nosewise? You're alive!" A young girl's voice spun us all around. She dropped her tray of foamy mugs and spilled the suds across the tavern floor, turning half a dozen heads.

"So much for unnoticed," Morgana murmured.

"G-G-Guinevere," Arthur croaked. His face went flush and he stumbled back a step. Guinevere, the tavern keeper's daughter, a willowy girl with short brown hair, always had that effect on him. Though I could never work out why. I jumped up against her chest and licked her face. I hadn't seen her in months.

"Nosewise!" She laughed and pushed me away. "But

how? You survived the storm? And the soldiers! They came back with wild tales! Father, look who it is!" she shouted to the burly man behind the bar.

"The boy and dog! You survived it!" Leodegrance was Guinevere's father and the owner of this tavern. He waved off a customer vying for his attention and stomped over to us. "I can't believe it!"

"This was a mistake, coming here." Morgana tugged on Merlin's robe and whispered in his ear, "We should go."

"I know you, too," Guinevere said, pointing at Morgana. "You were with the soldiers. And you're the old man Arthur was trying to find."

Merlin smiled wide and threw up his hands. "No, no. I'm afraid I don't know what you're talking about. We're simple travelers just looking to buy supplies and be on our way. We don't even need accommodation for the night." Merlin patted Leodegrance on the chest. "If we could just purchase some bread and cheese, we'll be out the door." He dropped a heavy handful of gold coins on the table. Leodegrance and Guinevere ignored him.

"Tell me, Arthur?" Guinevere said, probing him with her eyes. "Something happened on Avalon."

Arthur's lip quivered. His face went flush.

My ears perked, and I noticed that some of the other patrons near the bar were listening in. *Come on, Arthur,* I thought. *Don't mess this up.*

"Tell me," Guinevere said, drawing even nearer to his face. "I worried about you." She tenderly placed her hands on his shoulders, and Arthur spasmed at her touch. His arms flailed and his legs kicked at the floor and his whole body tumbled backward over the stool. Morgana gasped. Merlin reached out to catch him, but he was too late. Arthur crashed into the ale-soaked floorboards, and his cloth pack ripped in two.

The glimmering gold-and-silver blade of Excalibur cut through the fabric, and the sound caught the ears of every patron in the bar.

The sword slid away from Arthur and spun in the pools of ale, glimmering bright and lighting up the tavern with golden beams. Every eye beheld its light.

"That's . . . that's . . ." Guinevere trembled in awe and struggled to speak.

"The sword" was all Leodegrance could say. "The sword. The sword!"

"It's the sword!" someone cried.

"Excalibur!" shouted another.

"No, no, it isn't!" Arthur said, scrambling across the floorboards. "It's nothing." He grabbed Excalibur by the hilt and hastily tried to shove it back into his torn sack. But when he thrust it into the bag, the razor-sharp blade sliced the cloth to ribbons, which fell around him like streamers.

He was left holding the sword upright, down on one knee, in the most heroic pose I'd ever seen.

"Arthur, you *did* pull the sword from the stone," Guinevere said in almost a whisper. Her words swept across the silent tavern. No one spoke. Not Merlin nor Morgana. Least of all me, even though I was dying to. I was the one who'd really pulled the sword from the stone.

"Might I offer an explanation?" Merlin said. But his words were lost. The entire tavern rushed Arthur.

"He is our king!" Leodegrance cried, lifting Arthur up on his shoulders.

"King Arthur! King Arthur!" the awed patrons chanted. They ran up to the bar, completely ignoring Merlin, Morgana, and me. I had to leap and slither between their wet boots or else be crushed by their enthusiasm.

"That's what the soldiers feared," Leodegrance said, reverently placing Arthur on top of the bar. "Our king has been found. After these long years of chaos, a true king has returned to his people. Arthur!"

"Arthur! Arthur! Arthur!" they chanted.

"No, please," Arthur begged. "Don't call my name. I'm not the king—I swear it!"

"Arthur! Arthur! King! King!" they cried.

I saw Arthur panic. He looked for Merlin, but he'd been swept away by the crush of the crowd. Morgana was pinned between two tables. He spotted me down on the floor, dodging soggy boots. Arthur raised Excalibur high above his head; the golden light shone in bright beams, and all the patrons raised their heads. Arthur brought the sword down, hard into the thick oaken bar, and flaming splinters jumped up toward the ceiling. That got their attention.

"Listen to me!" he shouted.

"The king speaks," said a man in the crowd. Arthur looked exasperated.

"Please! I'm not the king," he said. "I didn't pull the sword from the stone."

Murmurs spread through the thick crowd. Between legs and long overcoats, I saw Leodegrance look up at Arthur. "Whoever pulls Excalibur from the stone should be our rightful king. If you didn't do it, then who did?"

Arthur grimaced and searched the crowd. He lowered his arm and pointed straight at me. "It was him!"

"Who? Who?" The patrons shouted and spun, trying to find the person at the other end of Arthur's pointed finger. They shoved against each other and searched the hall. But no one was looking down. I was on the floor pressed between their heavy boots. I squeezed between knees and climbed onto a tipped-over bench. From there I leapt up onto the wet bar and skidded to Arthur's side.

As I spun into his leg, I caught Merlin, in the corner of my eye, waving his hands wildly. He forcefully clapped his hand over his mouth and shook his head. *He told me not to make a scene.*

"Him!" Arthur placed his hand on my head. "Nosewise pulled the sword from the stone. If that makes you king, then he's the king."

"Oh, my stars," I heard Merlin groan.

The tavern dwellers went slack-jawed for a moment. Some looked to each other and some scratched their heads. Some were frightened. A wild-haired woman stepped forward and gave voice to their fears. "The king is mad!" she screeched.

"A mad king!" The cry went up through the hall. "A mad king!"

"No king is better than a mad king!" someone shouted.

"A dead king is better than a mad king!" cried another.

The tavern folk were in a frenzy. Violence was in their eyes. They rushed toward us. In the back of the hall, I saw Merlin grab his staff. *Don't make a scene,* he'd told me. Well, one look and I'd say a scene had already been made.

"Wait!" I shouted. "I did pull the sword from the stone. Some of you should know me. I'm Nosewise! I'm the wizard's dog, remember?"

All around the tavern, mouths hung open, but no words came out of them. Some of the patrons' hands were shaking. Others stood staring at me, wide-eyed. A few looked like they were about to scream.

"Wait!" An older, redheaded woman pushed her way through the crowd. Her hair was wrapped up in a tight bun, and her lips glistened. She swayed slightly and looked at me cross-eyed.

"I remember you, Nosewise!" she said, raising her sloshing tankard. Boy, did she smell like ale. "You've been here before. It's hard to believe *you're* the one who finally pulled Excalibur after all those brave men and women trying, but— *hic!*" She hiccupped violently and spilled some of her drink on her tunic. "But the more of these delicious ales I drink, the more sense it all makes. *Hic!*" With that she downed the rest of her enormous tankard and wiped her mouth. She turned to the patrons and said, slurring, "That dog is the king, you know."

"Hear! Hear! A very good point indeed!" Merlin rapped his staff on the floor and pushed through the crowd. "We'll tell you the whole tale. But to make it go down easier, the next round of drinks is on me." Merlin dumped his entire sack of gold out onto the bar. "There's enough here for the next three rounds. How does that sound?"

"Sounds pretty good," someone said.

"All right."

"I'll drink to that." The patrons were restless and confused. I wagged my tail at them.

Merlin pushed the tall pile of gold toward Leodegrance, who stood dumbfounded. "Barkeep, please. Help me!" he said. Leodegrance blinked and patted the gold, not quite knowing what to do with it. His eyes stayed on me.

"Don't be scared, Leody," I said, and he nodded slowly.

"The dog talks," Guinevere croaked. "He actually talks."

"I t-told you he d-did," Arthur stuttered to her. "Please help your father get the drinks. The crowd is restless."

Guinevere shivered and set to work, taking patrons' empty mugs and filling them with ale from the barrels behind the bar.

"My friends, we will tell you everything. But first we will have drinks. And we will have music." Merlin extended his walking staff to Morgana and gestured for her to take it.

"You want me to do it?" she asked, growing pale.

"You have a talent for this. Please," Merlin implored her.

Morgana nodded and took his staff. The glassy black Asteria stone set in its handle shimmered as Morgana took power from it. She pushed her way to the corner of the room, where a fiddle and bow rested on a high shelf. She closed her eyes and thought a very Certain thought to speed her magic, and long white tendrils slithered from the stone on the end of Merlin's staff.

The wisps took hold of the bow and fiddle and raised them in the air. Then they touched, and the bow pulled a long sweet note across one of the strings. The fiddle played itself.

"Amazing," one woman cooed.

"They are wizards," announced another.

"It's true," I said, puffing out my chest. "And we only use our magic for good!"

They tensed at my voice and gave me sour looks. Even with the music and the magic I scared them!

"Nosewise, better let me do the talking. Just for a while," Merlin said behind a cupped hand. Then he turned back to them. "Because we've got a lot of tale to tell!"

Merlin told them how he and Morgana had lived in a quiet house in the woods with their little dog, Nosewise. When Nosewise saw the spells they could weave—fire, lightning, invisibility—he became obsessed with magic. As a joke, Morgana slipped me one of the magic Asteria stones.

"That's why I can talk today!" I shouted over Merlin, and brandished the Asteria around my neck.

"It's astonishing!" Guinevere said as she handed out the last of the ale. "I've never seen anything like it."

"It's unnatural!" said a cranky old man in the back of the bar.

"That's what I thought too, at first!" Merlin said, raising his finger. "And I commanded Morgana to never let him near the Asteria again. But she didn't listen, which turned out to be a good thing."

Merlin took his staff back from Morgana and used the Asteria to conjure images in smoke of our little house in the woods. He told how Morgana trained me in magic at night. And how Oberon, an evil prince of the Fae peoples, attacked our home and kidnapped both him and Morgana. He left out the part about how Morgana mistakenly thought the Fae man was her father and helped him breach the magical barriers around our house. Probably partly to spare her feelings, and partly just to move the story along. We didn't have all night.

"Let me tell it from here!" I interrupted. "You don't know this part!"

Merlin nodded and took a step back. I told the tavern folk of my frantic search for Merlin and Morgana, sniffing their scents through the woods and all the way to a castle, where I met Arthur. The people in the crowd were still nervous when I talked, but as I got deeper into the story (and they got deeper into their drinks), I felt them warm to me. I told them how Arthur and I had crossed into the Otherworld, where the Fae people live, and tangled with Oberon there. And how we'd followed them all back to our world and to the very tavern in Laketown where we were tonight. Guinevere and Leody were entranced.

"After we borrowed a boat to search for Merlin and Morgana on the isle of Avalon, a storm shipwrecked us, and the Lady of the Lake appeared," I said.

"You met the Lady?" Guinevere asked, and quivered.

"I did! She saved Arthur's life! Her name is Nivian, you know. All of us are good friends with her."

That impressed the patrons. Everyone in Laketown thought very highly of the Lady. I told them how we found Oberon on the island. It turned out he wanted to use Merlin's magic to remove Excalibur from the stone. But the Lady had enchanted Excalibur, she said, so that "only a worthy soul who loves man and would never do him harm might take it."

"Whoever pulls the sword from the stone is king! King!" the redheaded woman shouted through her hiccups. No one seemed to think it strange that I could talk now. From the smell of the crowd, they were each on their third or fourth ale. And Merlin motioned for Leody and Guinevere to keep them coming.

"That's why Oberon wanted it," I said. "He thought if he could get the sword, it would make him king of man. And then he could make you all do whatever he wanted."

The crowd booed at that. I had them good.

I described Oberon's terrible worm sprites, and Merlin made their ghostly shapes in smoke. The worm sprites were foul creations Oberon had fashioned in the Otherworld. They ate magic. Casting spells at them was useless; they swallowed them into nothing and grew bigger. Oberon set two of them on me, and they chased me all through the woods, trying to swallow the Asteria on my neck. I led them through a tunnel under a mountain and shot a great force of magic at them. They swallowed it and grew so big they became stuck in the tunnel. I fed them more and more magic until they cracked the mountain's foundations and it collapsed on them. I barely escaped with my life.

"Wonderful, Nosewise!" Leody shouted, slapping his knee.

"Then I returned to fight Oberon!" I said. Every eye was on me and every ear was perked. "He forced Merlin to use his magic on the Sword in the Stone, but the power of the enchantment was killing him. I fought Oberon, his soldiers, and his last worm sprite with Arthur and Morgana beside me. When it seemed like we would lose, I told Arthur to try to pull the Sword in the Stone. But he couldn't. I leapt up to help him, and the moment I clamped Excalibur's hilt in my teeth, it slid out like nothing at all."

Everyone in the tavern gasped. "What then?" Leody shouted.

"Arthur picked up Excalibur and sliced the worm sprite in two. Oberon's soldiers fled. And with the last magic-eating worm sprite gone, Nivian, the Lady of the Lake, came to our rescue. She froze Oberon in ice and the day was won." I wagged my tail proudly.

A grizzled old man pushed forward and dropped to his knee. "King Nosewise!" he shouted.

"King Nosewise!" echoed a woman across the bar. Then everyone was on their knees, raising their half-empty mugs of ale. "King Nosewise! King Nosewise! King Nosewise!"

The rest of the evening passed in a blur. More men pulled out instruments and joined Morgana's magic violin. Some women fashioned a crown for me out of an old basket, but it kept falling off my head. Merlin kept people laughing with stories of his youth. Morgana led the folk in an enormous circle dance around the tavern. Arthur and Guinevere whispered and laughed together in a corner.

And people feasted. I hadn't seen so many racks of ribs and pork loins in my entire life. I went from table to table, begging for scraps. But I was King Nosewise now, and scraps weren't good enough for a king. People handed me whole ribs and giant cuts of meat. By the end of the night the room was spinning, and I collapsed on the thick carpet, my nose tingling in the warmth of the raging fire.

2

Waves of Doubt

WHEN I WOKE, THE FIRST LIGHT OF DAWN WAS PEEKING IN through the dirty windows. The tavern was as crowded as a dog kennel with men and women still snoozing on benches, under tables, and wrapped up in carpets. No one had made it home to bed.

The smell was thick. Unwashed armpits laid the foundation, and stale ale and putrid meats filled out the rest. I loved it.

I looked around the hall for my pack. Arthur and Guinevere were still on the sofa in the corner, but instead of chatting away like they'd been last night, they were leaning against the wall, asleep. I spotted Morgana on the upper balcony, dozing on a cot. Merlin was hunched over the bar and talking with Leodegrance. They were the only two awake.

"Our plans are far from settled," I heard Merlin say as I padded up to them. "Nosewise's magical training is still in progress, Arthur is an immature boy, and Morgana, while advanced for her age, lacks proper judgment. Add to that the fact that the Lady of the Lake has not yet instructed us on what we should *do* with Excalibur, and you will see our predicament."

"Good morning, Merlin!" I said, and leapt up on the bar. "Good morning, Leody!"

"Ahh!" Leody stumbled backward and nearly cracked his head on a shelf. "Oh, Nosewise. Hello, my—my king, should I call you?" He tried to bow, but Merlin stopped him.

"The Lady of the Lake never intended Excalibur to make its wielder king. Her enchantment merely released the sword to someone who would use its power to protect mankind. The whole kingship myth rose up around it."

"The Lady is really nice," I added. "Have you met her?"

"Um . . . no," Leody answered me, then turned to Merlin. "I'm not sure I'll ever get used to this. A talking dog."

"You will," Merlin replied. "But maybe not today. The ale helped our cause last night. But in the cold light of day, I fear what the Laketowners shall think."

"Should we sail back to Avalon?" I asked Merlin. "And tell the Lady about our party?"

"Yes, Nosewise," he answered. "But maybe don't tell her quite everything—Excalibur coming out of Arthur's pack, and King Nosewise, and all that. Hopefully, the tavern folk will consider it all a dream."

"It still seems a dream," Leody said.

"Good!" Merlin answered.

"Except for the talking dog before me."

"Perhaps you might leave him out, if questioned," Merlin said. "Now, please gather our supplies while we wake our companions. Nosewise, come along."

I followed Merlin as he went up the stairs to wake Morgana, but behind his back I whispered to Leody, "Don't forget the part about the talking dog!"

I licked Morgana's cheeks and she woke easily, but Arthur was harder to get up. "Arthur! Arthur!" Merlin whispered, and Morgana came down and poked him in the chest.

"Get up!" she commanded.

I jumped on his lap and licked his chin. His head wobbled back and forth as I pressed him with my snout. His whole face was shiny with my slobber by the time he roused, saying, "Nosewise, get off!"

"Finally awake," Morgana said. "We have to go!"

Arthur's eyes were wide, but he seemed paralyzed. His gaze was fixed on Guinevere's head resting on his shoulder. "She . . . I . . . Guin . . ."

"Yes, she fell asleep against you. It's very romantic. But we need to leave now," Morgana said.

Behind us, Leody was laughing. He put down a big burlap sack that smelled of cheeses, breads, and meat, and gently lifted his daughter in his arms. "He's always had an eye for Guiney, this one," he said. "I'll bet he never washes that shoulder again."

"He better wash it," Guinevere said sleepily. "Every time I see him, he smells like onions." Morgana and Merlin couldn't help but laugh.

We made it to the dock just as the sun topped the horizon, and Guinevere and Leody got their first glimpse of our boat.

"Well, I'll be!" Leody said, "It's entirely green!"

"Made of weeds and vines. How can it be?" Guinevere asked.

"It's made of the Lady's magic!" I answered them, wagging my tail. "I was there when she grew it up from the lake. Vines, reeds, leaves, and tendrils all came together, dripping with magic!"

Our seaweed boat bobbed in the harbor. The early light glistened off the leafy mesh that made up its sails, and the thick reed that formed the mast bent gently in the wind. It was much more beautiful than any of the dead wooden boats moored about it, and it smelled like Lady Nivian. Even from the end of the dock I could smell her magic, as if it were right beside me.

"I can't believe you met the Lady," Guinevere said to us.

"Can't believe a lot of things," Leody echoed.

"What was she like?" asked Guinevere.

"She's kind and generous and smells like lavender," I answered.

"She's my idol," Morgana said.

"A good teacher," Merlin added.

"She's scary. I watched her freeze her brother solid in ice," Arthur answered. The three of us glared at him. "Well, she is, but for a Fae she's nice. Which isn't saying much, because every other Fae I've met has been evil."

"Arthur's just a scaredy-cat," I said as we approached the boat. "Nivian saved all our lives. You should come with us and meet her!"

"Perhaps another time," Merlin said, stepping between us. "For your help, thank you. But now we must take advice from our great lady. Please help the people of your town forget what they saw last night. We are not prepared to face the wider world yet."

"You have my word, Master Merlin. Children, good voyage." Leody dropped the supplies in the boat and shook Merlin's hand. He slapped Arthur on the back and bowed to Morgana. He didn't quite know what to do with me, so I pushed my head into his hand and let him pet me. "Good boy, Nosewise," he said.

"Bye, Leody! Bye, Guinevere!" I said, and licked their faces. "Visit us soon!"

Merlin shooed me into the seaweed boat as the rest of them said their goodbyes. Leody untied us and pushed our boat off the dock while Merlin filled the sails with conjured wind. We sailed away from Laketown and our friends just as the rising sun's light filled the streets and the townspeople stepped out to begin their day.

Arthur seemed depressed.

"What's wrong, chum?" Morgana asked him. "Missing your girl?"

"She's not my girl," Arthur said, irritated. "She's just a friend."

"Yeah, but you *like* her," Morgana said in a singsong voice.

"I like her too," I offered. Guinevere was very nice.

"But not like Arthur does," Morgana said, poking him. He swatted at her hand. I had no idea what they were squabbling about.

Merlin chuckled. "It was good to get away." The crisp, cool air blew his hair and beard in a tangle from his face, and he smiled cheek to cheek. "Perhaps not entirely to plan. But we secured food and supplies and got to feel the summer air. I'm sure the Lady appreciated our time away as well."

I cocked my head. "Why would the Lady want us to leave?" I asked.

"Well, as much as she loves our company, we have been practicing magic an awful lot on her island."

"Ah yes," Morgana said, turning from Arthur. "And our Asterias draw magic from the world around us. That's why they're so much more powerful on Avalon. They draw from Nivian's magic."

"But she's so strong," I said. "How could our little magic bother her?"

"A good question," Merlin said, raising an eyebrow. "But nonetheless, she's confided in me that she's felt quite exhausted of late. Positively drained."

"Drained," I repeated aloud. Something about the word was frightening to me. "How could she be *drained* by only us?"

Crack! Boom!

An echoing rupture sounded over the surface of the lake, and all our conversation stopped.

"What was that?" Arthur asked, piqued.

"I don't know," Merlin answered. "It was loud."

"Nosewise has the best ears," Morgana said. "What was it?"

"Rock and ice breaking. Rumbling down a hill." I perked my ears toward the island and cupped them. "There's something faint. Like scratching."

"Maybe the Lady is doing work on the island," Arthur offered. "Maybe she's making a better prison for Oberon."

"Why would she do that without us?" I said. "We should help with that."

Merlin looked annoyed with him. "I don't think that's the case. She would only take up major work in an emergency."

"An emergency?" Morgana said. "You think something's gone bad with Oberon?" The color left her face, and I saw her reach for her wrist, the place her Asteria had last been kept. My own Asteria began to glow.

Shriek!

A high-pitched cry cut through the air. It was a familiar sound.

I found my Certainty: *I will protect my lady.* I jumped down off the reedy bench and took up a spot next to Merlin behind the sail. A great wind blew through my Asteria and sped the boat. "We need to go faster!"

"Nosewise, what did you hear?" Morgana asked me.

"A shriek," I answered, and she went pale. Merlin's eyes popped, and he redoubled his magic wind. With the two of us filling the sail at full strength, the boat rocketed across the water, chopping hard into the waves and bouncing.

"Don't you think we're going a little fast?" Arthur shouted over the wind.

"I heard a worm sprite!" I shouted back at him.

"W-worm sprite?" Arthur said, almost too quiet to hear over the crashing boat and howling wind. "But—but we killed them all. One with Excalibur and the others under the mountain."

25

The mountain. The two big worm sprites chased me there. And I killed them.

Or so I'd thought.

From the looks on my pack mates' faces, I could tell they were thinking the same as me. What if the mountain hadn't killed the worms, but had only trapped them? All of Avalon was ripe with magic. Had they been feasting on it from within the mountain? Maybe the Lady wasn't feeling weak from our magic but because the monstrous worm sprites were leeching her magic dry.

I heard another shriek.

None of us spoke for what seemed an hour. Merlin and I were dead set on the sail of the boat, pushing it as fast as we could without capsizing us. He used his hands to show me when he wanted more wind or less. Behind us, Arthur and Morgana steadied the hard-reed tiller, working furiously to keep the boat righted and sailing true.

By the time the shores of Avalon came into view, both children were audibly panting from the strain. Merlin's hands were shaking, and my winds were blowing wild. *We're close,* I told myself. *We need to keep going just a little longer. . . .*

"Oh, stars!" I heard Arthur shout behind me. I turned and saw him and Morgana holding a limp black cord. She gasped as it turned to mush in her hands. The hard-reed tiller was gone. Morgana fell into one seaweed wall, and Arthur sank into a mound of wet rot. The boat's bottom darkened and sagged into the water. Lady Nivian's creation was dying.

Merlin froze the rotting sections solid with cold magic, but new rot crept out from the old and dropped the icy blocks into the lake. Morgana grabbed Arthur just as the frozen vines beneath his feet disappeared, and dragged him up past the mast of the boat. Merlin and I followed them to the prow. Avalon wasn't far off, but the waves were rough and crashing violently into the shore. Suddenly we were rising into the sky. I turned back in horror to see the mast and rotten sail fall away from us. The front of the boat flipped over and forced us all down deep into the sludgy waters. My vision went gray, and cold slime filled my mouth. I kicked and tried to swim, but in the murk I couldn't tell which way was up. Bubbles streamed from my nose and bounced all around me, finally guiding me up to the surface. I broke through at the base of a strong, cold wave but was forced down again, spinning in the icy waters.

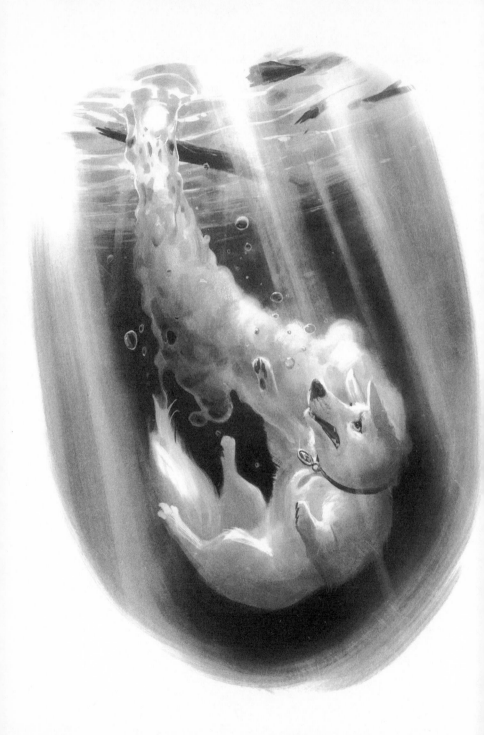

3

The Worms Return

A BLURRY BLUE SKY WAS THE FIRST THING TO COME ACROSS MY eyes. Buzzing through it was a glowing spot. The spot stretched into a string as my eyes focused on it, and I watched it spiral down, down toward my chest. It slipped below my nose and I lost track of it, but something vibrated at my neck, and I craned down to look. My Asteria was nestled in the wet fur of my mane, but it was dark. A thin, wiry worm stretched against it and glowed brighter and brighter.

Then two wet fingers pincered the worm and yanked. The little strand held on to my Asteria and pulled taut before popping off.

I blinked and saw Morgana standing over me. "Are you hurt?" she asked.

I remembered struggling through the goopy waters and dizzily washing up on the shore of Avalon. I stretched my neck and legs, then rolled over on my belly. The snow below my paws was warm. I sniffed it and realized that it wasn't snow at all, but fine white sand. I raised my head and looked up the shore. There was no snow or ice on the beach, just sand and patches of brown grass. Morgana was struggling with something above me. The little glowing worm was darting though the air as Morgana swatted at it, shooing it away from my neck. "Arthur! Help me with this!" she shouted, and he jogged into the space above my head.

"What do you want me to do?" Arthur asked in a panic.

"The sword!" Morgana commanded. "It's a worm sprite!"

A *worm sprite?* I thought. Oberon's flying creatures had grown huge on the magic of this island. They hadn't been this small since they'd first attacked us at Merlin's home in the woods. *These must be babies,* I thought in horror, and scrambled to get away as Arthur pulled Excalibur from its soggy woolen sheath.

The tiny worm sprite buzzed away from Morgana and made a beeline toward me. I barked and accidentally brought a spark of magic to the surface of my Asteria. The worm wiggled with excitement. I ran a wide circle in the sand and hid behind Arthur just as the glowing blade of Excalibur rose above the wool.

Fizzle pop! sounded on the other side of Arthur, and I peeked my head around. Fine white vapor rose up from the sword. "There's one to the right," Morgana said, pointing.

I turned and saw a sprite as thick as an earthworm spiraling toward us through the sky. Morgana stepped away and Arthur swung the sword, wincing and covering his eyes. But Excalibur guided itself to the center of the worm sprite, splitting it into two brief flames.

"Where are they coming from?" I asked Morgana. She knew the most about the worm sprites from her time in the court of the Summer Fae.

"I don't know," she said. "I thought they only made three."

"And I thought we killed them all," I said, lowering my chin to protect my Asteria. The Summer Fae had corrupted three ordinary sprites to make them feed on magic. I'd watched Arthur kill one that had grown enormous at the altar of the Sword in the Stone. And I'd crushed the other two under a mountain of ice. So where were these little ones coming from?

Arthur killed another as Morgana helped Merlin up from the sand. He extended his staff to her and she grabbed it to balance him. There was a glowing worm attached to his Asteria in the handle, and the creature vibrated stiffly. Once Merlin was back on his feet, Arthur lifted the blade to the sprite and burned it away.

"What's happening, Merlin?" I asked. "The snow is all melted, and little worm sprites are everywhere."

"The magic of this place is withering," Merlin whispered hoarsely.

A roar sounded over the hills, and my fur stood on end. I knew that sound. My ears cupped in the precise direction of the cry, and I barked. Without thinking, I bolted up the beach, my pack trailing behind me.

Our journey toward the source of the roar was frustrating. Merlin was so slow, it took him forever to navigate the wet stone and dead grass that had appeared everywhere on the island.

"Where is all the snow?" I shouted, sniffing the ground while I waited for Merlin to catch up. My master panted and pressed his long staff into the soggy ground, moving as quickly as he could.

"Isn't the Lady's magic what makes the snow?" Arthur asked jogging up to me.

Morgana and Merlin traded dour looks.

"The boat fell apart too," Arthur said.

My chest tightened and my ears shot up straight. "I've got to find the Lady!" I shouted, and charged off over the spongy grounds.

"Nosewise, wait!" Merlin called, and Morgana echoed him.

I didn't know what I was looking at. I'd passed a thick stand of trees on top of a hill and glanced down at the valley below. The island was unfamiliar to me without the snow, but something very strange was happening on the valley floor.

Two rivers made of stone flowed up from the center of the valley, rose in the air, and thrashed against the ground. But rivers didn't rise into the air, and they were never made of stone. So that wasn't what they were.

They were worm sprites, grown large. But not as large as trees, the way I'd seen them before. They were as large as roads, as thick as the tower of Lord Destrian's castle. As big as the biggest things I'd ever seen.

But where were their heads? All I saw were tails and two slowly undulating bodies that came to meet in the valley's center. They pressed together there and disappeared. Had they been beheaded? Was the Lady triumphant?

Behind me I heard squishy footsteps and words of encouragement. I turned and saw Arthur and Morgana, each standing at Merlin's side, helping him over the fallen branches.

I ran to them. "Nosewise!" Merlin murmured, and reached out a hand to me. I gave him a lick and jumped onto my hind legs.

"I've found them! The Lady's killed them!" I said, leaping. "They're down in the valley. They've got no heads!"

Merlin gave me a hopeful glance, and Arthur sighed with relief. Morgana stayed stony-faced. She made sure Merlin was steady with Arthur. "Show me," she said.

I led her through the stand of trees to the top of the hill. We looked down into the valley, and I barked in the direction of the stone rivers beneath us.

My woof bounced against the side of the other hill and echoed back to us.

Then the stone rivers started to writhe.

"Nosewise . . . ," Morgana said.

Their gigantic tails wiggled and swam backward. A grinding, churning sound erupted from the place where the headless worm bodies met. Dirt exploded around them, and the tails stretched back farther and farther.

"Nosewise, they aren't headless!" Morgana said.

The ground exploded, and two enormous, frothing faces took to the air, one white, one coal black. They'd been burrowing in the dirt. Not dead, only half-buried. They looked up the hill at me, and by their eyes I could tell: *they remembered.*

"Arthur, the sword!" I shouted, running back into the stand of trees where he was helping Merlin.

"I know—I've got it!" Arthur said, brandishing Excalibur and squinting with concentration at a teeny-tiny worm sprite that was circling Merlin's Asteria. He swiped, and the blade cut the baby worm to vapor.

"I've a talent for this," Arthur said, sheathing the sword in its woolen scabbard.

"No!" I shouted. "There are more!"

"More?" Arthur asked with a showy unsheathing. "Well, present them to me. These worms are no match for the blade."

Above our heads there was a screech, and we all looked to the sky. Everything blue had been blocked out. All we saw was coal black and stark white, and glowing eyes, sharp teeth, and heaving, steaming gills.

"These worms are big," I said.

Arthur screamed and crouched with the sword above his head as the ash-white worm spiraled down to us. Just as the sprite's open jaws were over Arthur's head, Merlin blasted a furious, golden flame that vaporized a patch of trees downwind of him. The scent of the magic was pure and strong, and the titanic worm sprite turned to see. Its skull slid through the air and barely missed crushing Arthur. Its thundering body followed, a few feet above him.

The sword shot up straight. Arthur's arms looked possessed as they thrust the silver blade into the sprite's white belly. Blinding lights flashed, and I felt heat against my closed eyelids. When I opened them again, I saw that the sword was out of Arthur's hands and lodged in the worm sprite's flying form, like a glowing needle in the belly of a bull.

The enormous worm spasmed, and waves of shock rippled out to its tail. Then it fell, crushing trees and shaking the hill. The white worm went silent, dead, but above our

heads there was another screech. The black worm floated above the trees, casting shadows down on all of us.

"Retrieve the sword!" Merlin called out, and readied his staff. The black worm began a slow descent, and Merlin sent an orb of light into the trees to distract it. "Fetch it now!"

Arthur, Morgana, and I raced to the resting body of the gigantic worm. Its carcass stretched across the entire summit of the hill. "The cut was up here!" Morgana shouted, running to a place right behind the worm's door-sized gills. She slapped her hands against its side and tried to reach beneath.

"Where is it?" Arthur asked, scanning the creature.

"I think it fell on it," Morgana replied. She'd gotten down to the ground and was trying to heave the monster up with her back. "Help me!"

Arthur dropped to a crouch and tried to push with her, but it was like trying to move a mountain.

"I'll use shock!" I said. "Get back!"

Morgana and Arthur both dove out of the way as I dropped into my Mind's Nose and prepared myself for a great blast of force. I tried to harness the magical energies of the island as I'd done before and deliver a powerful push. But nothing seemed to rush up from the ground into my legs. I tried to focus my Asteria, but it felt weak and empty. This was nothing like when I'd fought the worms the first time. Then I'd felt all the power of the Lady's magic beneath me, lifting me up.

Now the ground felt dead.

I barked a blast, but it was hardly enough to knock a man off his feet. The gigantic worm sat still as a boulder. I barked my magic again and again, but there was no power in it. The island was eerily silent. A panic rose in me when I thought of the Lady.

Explosions sounded to my left. Merlin's magic was still working, at least, and he desperately blasted spells to hold off the black worm sprite. The monster was wary of him. It had just seen us kill its mate. It bit into Merlin's magic cautiously, sizing up the threat. I feared it would grow bolder and swallow Merlin whole with his Asteria.

Arthur and Morgana were clawing at dirt just underneath the worm sprite's body, digging for the sword. I launched myself at the ground with them, but the soil was rocky and full of clay. My toes yelped in pain when they hit sharp pebbles, and we made no progress. I glanced back at the black worm. It was drawing closer to Merlin, eating his spells with less interest. Its eyes were fixed on the glowing stone on top of his staff.

I heard a hiss, and turned to see that the dead white worm's gills were partly open and spewing a shimmering vapor. I sniffed and recognized the smell: silver and gold, laced with magic. Excalibur was buried within.

"Keep digging!" Morgana commanded me. "Nosewise!"

she called, but her voice faded as I pushed my head into the slippery gills.

Soft, wet flesh pressed against my ears, but there was light. The shimmering blade cast a glow against the inside of the worm sprite's belly. The walls of its flesh were smooth, marked by strange patterns, and slowly collapsing. The ceiling of the worm sprite's back was cracked and buckling down toward my head.

I trotted through the hardening flesh and vapor that made up the worm's guts and stopped at the blade of the sword. Excalibur hummed and chimed, and I looked for a place to bite that wasn't sharp. The hilt and handle were buried in the bottom side of the worm, and only the blade was accessible. I gingerly bit the flat end and tried to keep my tongue away from the sharp edge.

The sword felt impossibly light to me, and with no effort at all I dislodged it from the flesh. *The Sword in the Worm Sprite,* I thought, and took it by the hilt. I ran back to the place where the gills had been, but they'd closed and disappeared. The ceiling of the worm was falling rapidly now, and as I searched for a way out, the heavy-looking flesh collapsed on top of me.

I panicked and ran in a quick circle. Sunlight beat down on my head, and I saw that the sword had cut away the worm and I was standing on a deflated and dissolving skin.

I searched the trees for Merlin. A great shadow had fallen over the forest. The black worm sprite was descending, and in the wind and thunder of its flight, I heard a scream.

Some power surged through me. It connected my Asteria to Excalibur in my mouth, and the sword rang like a bell.

The dark shadow over the forest turned and revealed its face. The black worm sprite's eyes glowed white at the sight of the sword, or of me; I couldn't tell. But I had its interest. The great worm shrieked and slid through the air toward me, further crushing broken tree trunks and churning up dirt with its dragging belly.

My tail was between my legs and my ears were flat on my head, but I forced them upright. I willed my legs to move. I pushed the ground away from me behind my feet and hurtled forward at the worm sprite, cutting through the fear that made the air as thick as molasses. I passed Morgana and Arthur, who screamed at the lumbering monster.

There was no magic lifting me up from the core of the island. I couldn't feel the Lady's presence. But some power urged me forward with the sword in my mouth. It came from a hidden source—not Excalibur, not the Asteria, but a place that had been mysterious once, that I'd worked hard to make familiar.

It came from inside me.

4

⤜✕⤛

Dark Places, Dark Faces

THE COAL-BLACK WORM SPRITE WAS DEAD. WE'D CHARGED EACH other, and Excalibur had ended up in its head. Then it was over. The white was halfway misted into vapor and the black was dissolving quickly.

Morgana scooped me up in her arms. "Nosewise!" I was winded, and my chest ached from being thrown against the ground.

"Where's Merlin?" I asked.

"I'm here," a voice called from the woods. I lifted my head and saw Merlin hobbling his way through the broken trees. Morgana moved to assist him, but he raised his hand. "Stay with Nosewise. He's our hero."

I didn't feel heroic. The world wasn't saved. The worms had drained my beloved Avalon of all its magic.

Merlin tried to smile, but he could only grimace. He and Morgana exchanged a silent glance. Both sat beside me and stroked my mane.

After a while, Arthur appeared from behind the broken trees. He'd been fetching Excalibur from the black worm sprite's head. He was winded, and white with shock. He held the sword close to his chest, and I watched him strike at some tiny worms that flew into his path. One latched on to my Asteria. The tiny thing glowed and vibrated as it sucked what little magic it could from the stone. Merlin, Morgana, and I could only watch, exhausted.

"Why are you letting it do that?" Arthur shouted, running up to us. He crouched down and carefully pressed the edge of the blade to the baby sprite, evaporating it. Yellow smoke rose up between us. "Are you crazy? Did you want it to grow as big as those things?" Arthur pointed to the giant worm sprites that lay around us, disappearing into mist.

"It would take a long time," Morgana said flatly.

"Yes," Merlin murmured. "They must have been feeding for months."

My ears pressed against my head, and I reached down and bit my paws, though they weren't itching.

I'd left those worm sprites in the center of the mountain. I hadn't told anyone they might not be dead. They'd been feeding there. The Lady had complained of feeling weak. They'd been eating her magic and she hadn't even known.

Now all the magic was gone from the island. But where was Lady Nivian?

"We should look in that hole the worms were digging," Morgana said.

"What hole?" Merlin asked.

"They were burrowing in the center of the valley," she answered. Merlin blinked, and his mouth tensed.

"What do you think they were doing?" I asked, feeling panic rise in my throat.

"We'll have to go and see," Merlin said. He took hold of Arthur's hand and pulled himself up. I rolled to my feet, and the four of us walked through the splintered remains of the forest. The coal-black worm sprite hissed through its gills in a sickening way as it dissolved. All of us tried to ignore it.

"That's it there," Morgana said, pointing to the enormous cavern the worm sprites had burrowed at the base of the valley. The hole was deep and dark, and all around were torn-up piles of rock and clay.

"Is that what they normally do?" Arthur asked no one in particular.

"Sprites in their natural state do not dig," Merlin answered. "But these are no ordinary sprites. They are abominations, and I cannot say what would be their normal behavior."

"I never saw them dig," Morgana offered as we began to descend. "I traveled with them for weeks when they were

small. I saw them fly, eat magic, and rest. They never burrowed."

"Maybe they were digging for something," Arthur
said absently. The three of us turned to him, stone-faced.
"What?" Arthur said defensively.

We descended the side of the hill. I had a sickening feeling about what we'd find at the bottom of the burrow.

At the lip of the cavern, Merlin set his Asteria to cast a
bright white light. The dark depths were illuminated, and
my eyes widened.

Enormous blocks of ice vibrated, melting and refreezing
before us in undulating waves. Snow flurries swirled in ice-
cold wind, then suddenly vanished. Tree roots groaned and
grew up from the dirt, then cracked and rotted to dust.

"Something bad has happened here," Merlin intoned.

"It's the Lady," I said. "I knew it—she's hurt."

"This is wild Winter magic, and Summer," Merlin said.

"Oberon," Morgana gasped.

"Come close to me." Merlin pulled us near him. "These
energies are dangerous. We need protection."

"Why is this happening?" I demanded.

"Patience, Nosewise," Merlin answered. "We'll find out
soon."

A tingle spread through my paws, bones, and fur. A

bubble of watery magic grew out from Merlin's staff and engulfed our pack. It blocked the chill of the wind, and everything outside the bubble blurred. I tried to sniff, but the only smells I could detect were the four of us and Merlin's magic.

"Stay within the barrier," Merlin told us, and we began to walk. The ceiling of the cavern sparkled with melting ice crystals, which poured down over the dome of Merlin's shield. Along the ground, I watched them reform and freeze weeds and roots, which sprouted from the dirt at an unnatural rate. A wall of wildflowers burst into being at my right and ran up the ceiling of the cavern. They opened as quick as a blink, and their sweet fragrance overwhelmed me.

"Merlin, a scent is getting through," I said.

He held up a hand to stop us and examined the surface of the protective bubble. "Arthur," he said, pointing behind me. "We need your sword."

I spun around and saw that one of the baby worm sprites was chewing a hole in the bubble like a caterpillar working on a leaf. Arthur nodded and unsheathed the sword. He stabbed at the tiny sprite, and it went up in a puff of smoke. Merlin's bubble healed itself, and the scent of the wildflowers disappeared.

We continued our descent down the cavern. All around us magic was growing and contracting. Another baby worm sprite latched on to the protective bubble, and Arthur dispatched it.

"Why are they coming for us?" I asked. "There's so much magic around."

"Ours is fresh," Merlin answered. "All this"—he gestured to the shattering ice crystals and writhing roots—"is power in its death throes." He glanced at me grimly.

Farther down, the crackling ice and snow hardened against the walls of the cavern. Gnarled tree roots weaved through the frozen wastes, and then they were quiet too. Nothing grew; nothing changed; all was still.

"Seems safer here," Merlin murmured, and he dropped the protective shield that surrounded us. My toe pads made contact with the snow beneath my feet, but it wasn't cold, only hard like stone.

"Merlin, look," Morgana said, pointing up. Merlin raised his glowing staff to the high ceiling of the cave. The glassy surfaces refracted the rays of magic light and cast faint shadows on the walls. Smooth, curved ice rose high and caught the beams in swells and dips. It looked like a kind of sculpture.

A woman's face was cast in the ice and fixed to the highest part of the wall. Her forehead and nose were smooth and transparent, but a long, violent crack ran through her mouth and broke it into three shattered fragments. Beneath the face was a rough body of crumbling ice and snow. Crystal veins snaked along the walls behind her head and looked something like hair.

"Nivian!" I shouted, and ran to the figure. She was as tall as a house, and even when I jumped my highest, I couldn't get up past her frozen knee.

"What is it, Merlin? A . . . a statue like we found with the sword?" Arthur asked. Excalibur had once been held by a figure carved in rock that had looked just like Nivian. But the rock had actually been Nivian herself, or some aspect of her, and when I pulled Excalibur from the stone, she burst out of it and saved us from Oberon.

"That was no statue, and this is neither," Merlin said with a heavy heart.

The scent of the ice was Nivian, but her essence wasn't as clear and sharp as a rose anymore.

"She's bound in it!" I shouted. "Like she was with the sword! She's trapped in there, Merlin. We have to free her!"

Merlin avoided my eyes and approached the towering ice figure. He waved his staff before her chest, and I watched the light bounce through her.

"If it's an enchantment, we can break it," Morgana said, laying her hands on the Lady's shin. "Cool, but not cold," she remarked.

"Will the sword help?" Arthur asked, and Merlin turned to him. "It's what made the difference last time, I think."

"Excalibur cannot help us here," Merlin said, and waved Arthur away.

"What do we do, Merlin?" I asked. "If there's something

I can get, a potion from the house, an herb from the wood, tell me and I'll run out and fetch it."

"Something to break the spell? An unbinding element?" Morgana said hopefully.

"There is no spell here," Merlin said. He dropped the light below his beard, and his lips cast thick shadows up his face.

My Mind's Nose tingled, and my own Asteria glowed dimly. "It's a curse," I said. "Then we'll find the one who cast it."

"We will," Morgana said, standing up straight by my side.

"We will," Arthur echoed, gripping Excalibur at his hips.

"There was no curse," Merlin said bitterly. "There is no magic at work here. No foe to fight. No herb to find."

The tone of his voice made my hair stand on end. I looked up at Nivian's icy face. The long crack had broken her lips and turned them to crushed crystal, some shards of which had fallen to the floor.

"She's dead," Merlin said blankly.

"Dead?" Morgana spat the word from her mouth like a rotten piece of food.

"No!" I said. "She isn't!" I ran a tight circle around the snowy patch of rubble that had been her feet. I pressed my nose to the crumbling ice. *Spent magic.*

I smelled the stale essence of the Lady I loved, who'd saved us.

"How could she die? She's Fae!" Arthur demanded. "Fae are immortal!"

"Fae are *not* mortal," Merlin corrected him. "Time and injury may not slay them, but they are not eternal beings, forever promised their form. There are ways to make them die."

"What ways?" I said. "Who did this?"

"Ways beyond my understanding," Merlin said. He gripped his staff and dropped to his knees. His Asteria rested against her icy remains, and Merlin set his forehead beside it. He murmured something.

Tears welled in Morgana's eyes; she looked at me, horrified. Merlin was giving up. Merlin was saying Lady Nivian was dead. He ran his fingers against the ice and whispered wishes and sorrows.

"My lady." Morgana broke into a sob and fell to the ice beside Merlin. He placed a gentle hand on her shoulder and softly wept as well. Behind me, I heard Arthur's feet scrape against the crystals, and I turned to see him kneel and lay Excalibur against the broken ground.

A memory rose to the surface of my mind like a bubble from the bottom of the lake. I was standing on a cold raft, shivering with chill, the lifeless body of my boy laid below me. I howled and cried for help, bobbing around on the gentle waves. All hope was gone, but I still cried out.

"We can save her!" I said with a jolt. "Nivian brought

50

Arthur back to life on the lake. He was cold and gone, but she gave him life. She asked the water and the water said yes! We can bring her back!"

Arthur turned to me, gaunt. He had never fully accepted my story of what had happened on the lake. Merlin said people didn't like to hear about how they'd been dead. It made them uncomfortable, he said.

But I watched as Arthur's usual horror at my story transformed into hope. His grimace curled into a smile. "Brilliant!" he said. "We'll do for her what she did for me!"

I burst into a run and tackled Arthur. The two of us rolled merrily on the ground. Scratches and cuts from the hardened ice didn't bother me. This was all temporary; we would fix it soon. The Lady's soft hands would scratch my ears again, and I would lick them.

I tumbled to Merlin's feet and jumped up against his knee. "I saw how she did it, Merlin. She asked the water to return Arthur's life! How should I ask the water for Nivian?"

"There is no asking," Merlin said sharply. A hot tear flew from his eyelid and landed on my nose, startling me. "There are no words to 'ask the water.' Lady Nivian is a Fae, and an ancient one. Yes, she had power to work wonders on Arthur, just as a master carpenter might fix a wooden doll." He blinked hard and held the scruff of my neck. "But if that carpenter were to die, no matter what wonders he'd worked on his little doll, and no matter how much the doll wished it, that little man of wood could not save the carpenter's life.

"We are mortals, and the most gifted sorcerer among us is but a shadow in the life of a Fae like Nivian. There is no magic we have that could kill them, and there is nothing we can do to save them."

Merlin patted my head and slowly turned back to the Lady's broken form. He pressed his brow against the ice and resumed his mourning. Morgana was silent beside her occasional heaving, and Arthur remained on the floor of the cavern, his eyes downcast and unfocused.

I felt a slow rumbling deep in my chest. *The world breaking apart,* I thought, and rested my head on aching paws. My Asteria went black, and the four of us sat silent in the dark.

"Not mortal magic," a deep voice grumbled at my back. "That's right to say."

I raised my ears.

"But there is . . . one other way." The voice was half choked. I spun, and my Asteria illuminated a cloud of fragrant dust. Pollen and dandelion petals misted the air, and my light brightened the opposite wall of the cavern, where tangled and rotted lengths of root and branch formed the rough shape of a man. A tree man, who looked at me with hollow eyes.

The tree man wheezed and coughed. Dust and ash spewed from his mouth and caught the light.

"Oberon?" I said in shock.

Morgana whirled, and Arthur grabbed Excalibur. Merlin's Asteria ignited with hot white light, and the whole chamber was brightly lit. Behind the swirling clouds of pollen, a distraught face stretched high against the wall of the cave. Gnarled roots formed the shape of a mouth, and deep recesses hid dark eyes. Thick, trunklike wood made up the bulky shape of a body, and burned vines snaked out against the walls. Oberon's form looked lightning struck, scorched, diseased, and storm broken. Dead leaves, ash, and fungal rot rose in thick piles on the cavern floor.

"Prince of Summer, stay back!" Merlin shouted, brandishing his staff and letting off a threat of flames.

I barked a warning, and Arthur leveled his sword.

But Morgana walked past the three of us and approached the tortured shape.

"Morgana, stop!" I shouted, and started toward her. But she held her open hand back at me without turning. Stay! was the command, and old habits took over. I froze with my tail in the air and ears twitching.

Morgana ventured up the soft pile of decomposing debris beneath Oberon. Just like the Lady, he'd been stretched large and crushed against the side of the cavern. His face was crusty and still, but his dark eyes tracked down to Morgana, and I heard them scrape in their sockets.

"False father," Morgana said, looking back at him.

Oberon's mouth cracked as his knotty lips formed words. "False daughter."

"What did you do to Nivian?" she commanded.

"To Nivian, nothing, I . . ." Oberon struggled to speak. His voice was low and scratchy. "I would not wish my kin to die."

Oberon said it too. Did that mean she was really dead?

"Then what happened? Why are you like this?"

"The worm sprites that you slayed attacked us both down in the glade."

"The worm sprites!" I shouted, running up to Oberon's enormous form. "You *made* them!"

"Yes, you did," Morgana said. I glanced back at Merlin, but he kept his distance. Morgana had once thought of Oberon as her father and herself as half Fae. She'd lived with him for a time and knew him better than even Merlin did. "I watched you and Blodwen handle the sprites. They were bred to eat your enemies' magic. How could they have done this?"

"What mortals call magic and seek to control is what makes up the essence of a Faekind's soul. That's why you must focus the power through stones, while magic resides in our very bones." I could hear his mouth harden and crack as he spoke.

"And yet you bred sprites to consume it!" Merlin shouted, and stomped up to the tree man. "Foolish! Treacherous!" He thrust his staff at Oberon.

The tree man creaked but could not move.

"Foolish, yes. Arrogant, greedy. I tried to control them, but they cried out, 'Feed me!' When they were small, I was their master, but on this island they grew, and thus disaster. Their hunger insatiable, their strength unmatched, they fed in that mountain until it hatched."

"Inside the mountain?" Morgana asked.

My ears heated up, and I looked at her. "They *didn't* die," I said. "I thought they died in the mountain when it fell, but they didn't."

"This isn't your fault," Morgana said, laying a hand on my head.

"No," Merlin agreed, looking up at Oberon. "It's his."

"My fault, yes, my fault indeed. The mountain broke open and they came to feed. First on me they ate off the spell that my sister had used to bind me so well. I was freed but there was nowhere to go. They drained my power, first quick then slow. Nivian, sister, my ancient kin, came to my aid despite my sin. I told her, 'Flee! There's no saving us both.' Then the worms consumed us to fuel their growth."

Morgana and I traded a terrified look.

"We had no sword, nor mortal defense. When a sprite finds a meal, it never relents. They picked at us and drove us to ground. That awful scene is what you've found."

"But we killed the worms," Arthur said. "Can't your magic come back?"

"Drain a man of all his blood. Give it back. It does no good."

"Then how do we help Nivian?" I asked. "There's no mortal magic. Killing the worms didn't help. You said there was another way."

"What is it?" Morgana asked. "You did this to her; you must help us."

"To her, yes, but also to me. Soon I too will no longer be. She was the first to extinguish in mind. I will quickly follow behind."

"You want our help too," Merlin said snidely.

"That I wish, but do as you would. I won't stand in the way of my sister's good."

"Then out with it!" Merlin said. "How do we help her?"

"Do not accuse that I spin you a tale," Oberon said stiffly. I could see what a struggle it was for him to stay awake. "But I know where hides the Holy Grail."

Merlin gasped and my ears perked up.

"The holy what?" I exclaimed.

"The Grail of Life is left to rot, in the disappeared castle of Camelot."

"Camelot?" Arthur repeated with a hint of recognition.

"Camelot, that mortal capital, stands in the deep mists of the Fae realm's lands. Somewhere off in a dreamland's haunt, under the rule of Queen Mab, our aunt."

"No," Merlin whispered.

"A doorway there—" Oberon groaned, and the great trunk of his body split into two. Through the hole I saw a moonlit blizzard, and Otherworldly light filled the cavern.

"It's a portal," Morgana said.

"Where does it go?" I asked.

Merlin murmured amazedly, "The Winter Lands."

"Go! Find the Grail," Oberon bellowed with his final breath. "In this task, do not fail."

The great tree man sighed and turned gray. The split-open portal in his belly began to narrow.

"It's closing; we've got to go!" I shouted.

"Nosewise, wait!" said Merlin. "There's more to this story."

"We have to save Nivian," I cried. "I'm not giving up!" I leapt between the narrowly broken trunk into the Fae realm again.

PART II

5

The Woods of Winter

SNOW CRUNCHED BETWEEN MY TOE PADS. TREES HEAVY WITH ICE surrounded me. The cold was comforting. This was the Lady's land.

"Nosewise!" Morgana's voice sounded behind me, and I turned to see her crawling out from the roots of an old and gnarled tree. It was the way I'd come here too, I realized. I'd burst through the portal so fast, I hadn't managed to take it all in.

"Come on!" Morgana shouted from between a tremendous pair of roots. She reached her hand down and grabbed the hilt of Excalibur. She pulled up on the heavy sword, but the blade drew a line across a root in the old tree and split it in two. Sap gurgled from the broken root and spewed down on a mess of blond hair rising from the ground.

"Careful with that!" Arthur shouted as he held up his hand to the spouting sap. "What are you trying to do?"

"I'm trying to help you," Morgana said, dropping Excalibur in the snow. "It's just sap."

"Oh, it's bitter! And sticky!" Arthur yelled. He tried to clear the sap from his mouth and eyes but only succeeded at rubbing it deeper in.

"Enough!" a gruff voice shouted from below, and a quick bolt of light shot up and blackened the tree root, healing the break. "Boy, you're kicking mud in my eyes!"

Morgana grabbed the neck of Arthur's shirt and helped him scramble over the mess of roots.

I wagged my tail at them both and looked down at Merlin.

He was climbing away from the portal Oberon had made to the Otherworld, grasping at buried roots and laboriously lifting himself. He gave me a stern look.

Bad boy, said his eyes.

But his voice was measured. "You acted very quickly, Nosewise. Without much thought."

"The portal was closing quickly, Merlin. And Oberon said we could help Nivian. *That's* what I was thinking."

"He did say that," Merlin murmured. "Children, help me."

"Here, Master," Morgana said, bending down and hooking her arm through Merlin's.

"Just a minute—I've got to get this stuff out of my mouth," Arthur said. He was rubbing clumps of snow against his tongue and spitting repeatedly.

"Boy!" Merlin shouted.

"Yes, Master Merlin!" Arthur jumped to attention and helped lift him.

Merlin gasped and huffed as they dragged him over the knobby roots. "I'm all right. I've got it," Merlin said, standing and pushing them away. He gestured for Morgana to hand him his staff, and he balanced himself with it.

"Merlin," I said, wagging my tail, "we're in the Lady's land now, right? This is the Winter court. Where Nivian's family can help us."

Merlin grimaced at some pain in his hips and looked around. "Not the Winter court, but near it. These are their woods."

"Then they can help us," I said. "They'll take us to the Grail!"

"Was Oberon telling the truth?" Morgana asked. "Is there a way to save her?"

"The truth?" Merlin said. "Yes, mostly. Oberon always leaves some truth to be desired."

"The portal was closing," I said. "I had to go!"

Morgana started to say something to Merlin, but stopped herself. Merlin gestured for her to speak.

"That was our only door to the Otherworld, wasn't it? We can't make them on our own."

"No, we can't," Merlin answered.

"And even if Oberon told only part of the truth," I

said, "if there's at least a chance to save the Lady, I had to take it."

"I said you acted fast, my boy. Without much thought." He waved his hand so I would come near him. Then he bent and scratched my head. "Not that you acted wrongly."

I felt my body relax, and my tail wagged.

"There's much Oberon did not tell you," he said to Morgana and me. "I am not sure of this plan. But pondering it would have taken too long; the portal was closing. Maybe some good can be done on *this* side of it."

Merlin leaned close and whispered in my ear, "That's why we need you, Nosewise. Your conviction is your strength."

Joy bubbled up from my belly and filled my head. I leapt up and licked Merlin's scratchy face.

"I did a good thing!" I said happily, and Morgana laughed. Merlin stroked my head, and I looked over to Arthur.

There was a trampled patch of snow where he'd been standing moments before. I scanned the trees for him. "Arthur?"

I caught a scent on the wind; it was hair and spit, something like a wolf's, but different. My ears perked, and I caught growls, maybe half a dozen, followed by a yelp.

I charged through the snow, between a stand of trees, over a small hill, and down to him. Arthur stood near the edge of a clearing, surrounded on three sides by enormous wolves. He looked at me, frozen with fear. The path between him and me was open, so I sprinted to his side.

"Grrrrr!" I bared my teeth at the wolves as they enveloped me. Their huge white faces towered above; they were almost as tall as men. "Arthur!" I said through gritted teeth. "What are you doing here?"

"I—I—I, uh . . ." Arthur shook as he whipped his eyes between snarling teeth and stammered. "I had to relieve myself!"

The wolves' shoulders were raised; their tails were straight. They were readying for an attack.

"Why didn't you just do that near us?" I said.

"Nosewise, I don't have time to explain to you right now," Arthur said, teeth chattering. "This is bad. We have to run!"

"Don't run!" I said. "They'll chase you!"

The wolves were padding closer to us. My aggressive display hadn't scared them; it had just put them more on edge. Merlin and Morgana hadn't reached us yet. I could have tried to use my magic, but there were nearly a dozen of them, and I feared for Arthur.

I looked for the hunt in their eyes and didn't see it. At least they weren't hoping to eat us. It was more that they felt threatened. We needed to talk dog to them.

"Do exactly as I do!" I commanded. Then I hunched my back and dropped my tail deep between my legs.

Arthur grimaced and dropped down to all fours. He looked at me and I nodded my head toward my tail.

"I don't have a tail," he whispered.

"Just try!"

Arthur lifted an arm around his rear and let his hand fall between his back legs. If I could learn to speak his way, he could learn mine.

I glanced fleetingly at the wolves, making sure to avoid direct eye contact, and noticed that their shoulders were relaxing. Their tails were lowered, not all the way, but halfway between at ease and agitated.

"It's working," I whispered. "Now this!" I dropped on my back and rolled over to show my belly. This was a full submission. We'd had to submit more tentatively at first to make sure the wolves were seeing us as dogs. If they'd seen us as food, a full submission would only have been an invitation to rip our bellies out. When they relaxed their bodies, I knew they were listening to us, and we wouldn't have to run.

Three of the taller members of the pack trotted over to us. From the ground they looked even taller. Their long noses and thick jaw muscles crowded my view of the treetops.

"Wah!" Arthur screeched as a gray female dipped her snout down to his neck.

"That's a good thing!" I whispered.

The wolf sniffed his chest and belly. More gathered around us, four males and six females, with two others waiting outside the circle. The wolves took turns sniffing our necks, legs, and backsides. Arthur pushed a wolf away when she stuck her nose to his rear and sniffed. She shook her head, unsure whether to be angry.

"You have to let them," I said. "You want them to think we're a threat?"

Arthur closed his eyes and raised his legs slightly. The female wolf stuck her nose back into his butt.

It wasn't our turn to sniff their backsides; I had to show them I was sorry for growling first. But just because I couldn't smell them properly didn't mean I couldn't smell them.

These were healthy wolves. They smelled young, strong, and well fed. Their scent was off in that way that everything smelled off in the Fae realm, but they were close enough to ordinary wolves that I could recognize them. I hadn't ever met a wolf face to face before. But back when I lived in Merlin's house in the woods, I'd had long conversations with the pack that roamed beyond the wall of trees. We'd talk mostly through marks on trees and half-buried poop, but that was enough for us to know each other. They smelled me as I grew from puppy to dog, and I sensed their struggles through the seasons for food and dominance.

I liked wolves, and as this pack hovered over us, I had the sense of being embraced by old friends.

"How long does this go on?" Arthur asked as wolf snouts dipped into his ears and armpits.

"Until everyone feels comfortable," I said.

"Everyone except me," Arthur said.

Wolf heads began to rise. I saw them smile and pant.

"Let's get up very slowly," I said.

As I gradually rolled to my side, I heard a *crack!* and sparks rained down from above.

The wolves snapped to attention and searched for the source of the sound.

"Get away from them!" Morgana shouted. I jumped up to see her atop the small hill, holding Excalibur. She'd hacked it into a thick trunk, and the entire tree tipped forward and crashed to the ground, branches snapping loudly.

Hair raised on the wolves' backs and their tails went straight.

"Away!" Merlin shouted behind her. From his Asteria he spouted a tall torch of flames.

The big wolves fanned into a line, ready to defend us from Merlin and Morgana. Why were humans so stupid? Couldn't they see we'd befriended them?

"Go away!" I tried to say, but between Merlin's torch and Morgana's chopping trees, I couldn't be heard.

"What's happening?" Arthur shouted, huddled in a ball on the ground.

I tried to run out from behind the line of wolves, but a

large female at the end whipped around and grabbed me firmly by the scruff of my neck. She lifted me like I was a puppy again and set me between her legs.

Through the wolf's forepaws, I could see Merlin blowing huge towers of flame and Morgana fearfully waving the sword around her head. A wolf in the center of the line barked a command, and the whole pack charged them, leaving Arthur and me behind. I scrambled to catch up to their heels. Merlin's inferno was towering higher. Morgana was yelling. This would be a fiery, bloody battle.

But another voice shouted sharp and high above the rest. A whistle of icy wind that extinguished Merlin's flame.

The wolves stopped short, and I squeezed past the scratchy ribs of a pair of young males, eager to see what was going on.

A short, stocky woman stood wide-legged between Merlin and Morgana and the wolves. Her long hair was braided and knotted across her shoulders. She wore a jacket of woven reeds, and her tunic hung down to the snow.

"I think you better let go of that little stone of yours," she said to Merlin, in a pleasant but powerful voice. "The sword as well, pretty." Her hands still glowed with Winter magic. She was a Fae, and a strong one too.

Merlin and Morgana did as they were told. The woman turned to the wolves. She clicked her tongue and blew a kiss. Behind me, I heard tails wagging. The woman's face was round and kind. She looked young and old at the same time, like all Fae did. She turned back to Merlin and Morgana, her hands crackling with ice.

"Now, you had better tell me what you're doing, trespassing in the Lady's woods and agitating my wolves."

"I am Merlin!" Merlin said, raising his hands.

The Fae woman placed a hand on her hip and called, "Merlin the Wizard?"

"Yes, it is I," Merlin said, relieved.

"And what, may I ask, Merlin the Wizard, are you doing here?"

Merlin began to stump down the hill and gestured for Morgana to come with him.

"Stop!" the Fae woman said, and raised her hand. Merlin was knocked back as though he'd hit an invisible wall. Morgana caught him before he fell. "I did not bid you approach me. I asked your purpose."

Merlin composed himself. "Yes, Lady Fae, our purpose."

"Annaquin is my name, not Lady Fae. I am not of the Winter court."

"Anna—Annaquin, yes. In fact, I've heard of you," Merlin stammered.

"And I have heard of you, Wizard Merlin. But I have heard you're a friend. I wonder why a friend would bring fire to the Winter Woods."

"Annaquin, hear me!" Merlin shouted. "Lady Nivian, she's dead!"

Annaquin's confident demeanor melted away, and her voice broke. "What?"

"She was killed. Her essence eaten by worm sprites her brother Oberon made—"

"You speak the name of the traitor," Annaquin said. "You lie! Get out of these woods!" She whistled between her fingers.

All around, the wolves dropped into a crouch and growled. They paced up and flanked Annaquin. Her hands glowed bright with magic. "Out! Or we'll drive you out!"

"Wait!" I shouted, pressing between the big heads of two drooling wolves. Annaquin turned to me, and I pawed up to her. Some of the wolves by her side made way for me, which seemed to surprise her.

"And you are . . . ?"

"I'm Nosewise," I said, sitting at her feet. "What Merlin said is true. Lady Nivian died, but we're here to save her." I cried through my nose and Annaquin's face softened. She bent down to me and cupped my Asteria in her hand.

"This is her making," she said.

"The Lady gave it to me when I tried to help Merlin." I glanced at him and wagged my tail. "He loves the Lady. He brought fire because he thought I was in danger. He didn't understand the wolves were only trying to protect me. Your help is what we really need."

"My help? Why?" Annaquin asked.

"I . . . we need to find a grail!" I said. "I'm not sure why. Merlin knows why!" I tipped my head to him.

"We're searching for the Grail of Life. You must take us to Lady Mithriel, Nivian's younger cousin. She can aid us. The Grail is kept in—"

"I asked the dog the question, Wizard Man. Not you."

"Yes, but he's only—"

"He's not the one who brought fire in the Winter Woods. He has the Lady's charm around his neck. And besides"—she patted the head of a yellow-eyed female beside her—"my wolves like him. So, Nosewise, tell me, what can I do?"

After a bit of guessing to fill in the blanks of the plan, I convinced Annaquin to take us to Lady Mithriel as Merlin had said. I hadn't known Nivian had a cousin, but there had always been a lot I didn't know.

"Be good, my loves," Annaquin cooed to her wolves. She gestured for Merlin and Morgana to make their way down the hill.

"Thank you so—" Merlin started to say.

"Didn't ask you to speak, Fire Bringer," Annaquin interrupted. She turned to Morgana. "And who might you be?"

"M-Morgana," she stuttered. Annaquin was making everyone nervous.

"Apprentice to the apprentice. I've heard of you as well," she said. "Had a little trouble with the prince of Summer?"

Morgana blushed and nodded. "Ashamed to say."

"Don't be," Annaquin said with surprising tenderness. "That traitor would trick and lie and abuse the Great Mothers themselves if he thought it would get him what he wanted. Be angry, but not ashamed."

Morgana blinked a tear away. "I will."

"And I'm Arthur," Arthur said, finding the courage to stand up behind the pack of wolves. "I helped Nosewise on his way to the Sword in the Stone, and I wield it for him. I killed the worm sprites and fought off Oberon." A small smile crept across his face. "Have you heard of me?"

Annaquin looked at him and arched an eyebrow. "No," she said. "But that reminds me." Annaquin turned to Morgana. "Do you want to leave Excalibur sitting up there in the snow? Or are you going to bring it with us to see Lady Mithriel? I know some snow foxes that might love to have it!"

"Right!" Morgana said, running to fetch it. "Sorry, Lady Annaquin."

"Not a lady!" Annaquin called after her. "Not of the Winter court!"

Arthur was shrunken with embarrassment, and I padded over to him. Behind me I heard Annaquin say, "And you, Wizard Man, are you going to leave your glowing rock up there too? Don't you need it for your fire trick?"

I took Arthur's sleeve in my mouth and tugged him toward the pack. "She hasn't heard of me at all?" Arthur said. "Didn't I help?"

"You helped a lot!" I said through his shirtsleeve. "We couldn't have done it without you. But next time you have to pee, don't go off into the woods—just do it with us!"

Annaquin led us to a small clearing. Amid the roughly piled snow was a large wooden bench with two planks of polished wood jutting out from its base. Attached to the strange bench was a railing and two rows of hemp ropes strung with leather collars. *How'd this thing get into the middle of the woods?* I thought.

"You're dogsledding with dire wolves?" Merlin asked incredulously.

"It's called a wolf sled," Annaquin said. "And I'd prefer *you* to call it nothing, Fire Bringer. I've got my eye on you."

Merlin closed his mouth and nodded.

"So, the wolves pull you in that?" I asked Annaquin.

"I assure you they like it very much," she said. "One should never abuse a dire wolf. Not if one wants to keep one's fingers," she said, glancing at Merlin. He blanched.

"It looks fun!" I said, scampering off to where the collars lay. I pushed my nose into the snow beneath the collar in front and rose with the strap across my chest. It was a little big for me.

"That collar's about to eat you!" Annaquin laughed.

She gently lifted the too-large collar off my back and held it to her chest. "Sorry, that's Felan's spot. He's the leader."

A very tall dire wolf sauntered up to Annaquin and slipped his muscular neck through the collar. It fit him perfectly.

"What about those?" I asked, looking at the other harnesses in the snow.

"Taken as well. This is a dire-wolf sled. You'd be outpaced, little boy."

"Nosewise, come on." Morgana stood with Merlin and Arthur in the sled. "We shouldn't waste time."

I looked back at the pack of dire wolves as each slipped into a collar lined up before the sled. "It's not a waste of time," I mumbled as I stepped onto the sled by Morgana's feet.

Annaquin jumped up front, took the reins, and called, "Yah!"

The wolves broke into a sprint. Their powerful paws heaved us forward and sprayed snow in dizzying clumps. I could hear their happy panting echo across the frozen forest.

Why wasn't I allowed to run?

6

Bears, Queens, and Ice Castles

WE EMERGED FROM THE WOODS AT THE BASE OF A LONG SLOPING hill. All through the ride, the heavy canopy and thick tree trunks had obscured our view of where we were going. But music had been echoing off the trees for some time, growing louder and louder. It wasn't sad music befitting the death of someone as good as Lady Nivian, but happy, celebratory music. Whoever was playing it didn't know what had happened.

The castle rose high on the hill. It was composed of more than twenty tall towers, which all rose separately but were joined into a great hall at their lower halves, like a family of icicles grown thickly together. The towers were made of icy glass and sparkling gray stone. Dancing blue light flickered through the windows and lit up the entire castle. Hundreds of pinewood, ice, and packed-snow sleighs were circled about the main doors of the castle, and white bears and tall-shouldered elk were strapped into harnesses, waiting patiently.

"By the lights in the sky!" Merlin said, loud enough to be heard over the hiss of cutting snow and dire-wolf panting.

"Have you seen the Winter's Crystal before?" Annaquin asked over her shoulder.

"Only in my mind as I sat rapt by Lady Nivian's stories," Merlin answered, tears forming in his eyes. "Never in all my years did I think I would see the day when—"

"I was talking to the dog, Fire Bringer. When I'm talking to you, I'll let you know," Annaquin said, and Merlin closed his mouth. "Nosewise, have you seen it?"

I *liked* Annaquin. "I didn't even know the Lady had a castle!" I shouted over the noise. We were approaching quickly, and the sounds of jaunty music, braying draft animals, and commotion inside the castle made it hard to hear.

"Well, that's it!" Annaquin said with a nod. "The home of Lady Nivian and seat of the . . ." Annaquin winced as if she'd caught a lump in her throat. "The seat of the Winter court. It is an honor to serve there." She turned back to the castle and cracked the reins.

"Nosewise, we might be in for more than we bargained," Morgana whispered in my ear. "The Fae people are tricksters, and most don't have our best interests in mind. I spent time in the Summer court. They are not to be trusted."

"But those were Oberon's people," I protested. "Oberon's the bad one, not Lady Nivian. Her people will help us."

"Morgana is right to urge caution," Merlin said, hunching over. "Nivian is beloved to us, but she spends little time in the Otherworld. I studied with her on Avalon in my youth, and rarely did she leave the island to attend their affairs. Much of the rule has been delegated to her younger cousin, Lady Mithriel, whom I met once when I was fifteen. She is the one we must find."

"What?" Arthur yelled from the other side of the sled. He refused to let go of the railing and had been out of hearing range the entire ride. Morgana ignored him.

"But you do know her," Morgana said. "Do you think she'll be in the castle?"

"She is acting regent while Nivian is in our world. She is never far from the seat of power. Especially not on a night of celebration like this."

"What?" Arthur shouted again from the other side of the sled.

"They are not going to be happy when they hear about Nivian," Morgana said. My tail drooped between my legs. It was my fault she was dead.

"They don't need to be happy. We're not," Merlin said. "And still we fight for our mistress."

"What are you saying over there?" Arthur shouted. "I can't hear you!"

I stood and took a deep breath. "The Fae people are unhappy, but we're going to fight!" I barked back at him.

Arthur paled and turned to the rapidly approaching castle. *Fae people,* he mouthed.

The dire wolves planted their feet in the ice, and our sled skidded to a stop. Merlin, Morgana, and Arthur all held the rails, but lacking hands I tumbled into the snow. I rolled a few times and came to a stop at the base of a thick hairy leg. I looked up and saw two rows of sharp teeth growling at me. Beady black eyes squinted above a long square snout, and baggy cheeks hung below the teeth. An ice bear! It was raising its heavy paw to swat me down when a blur of white, black, and gray fur knocked it away. The dire-wolf pack was on him, and I scrambled out from beneath the storm of paws until I reached Merlin at the sled.

"Off! Order!" Annaquin was shouting. She was in the scrum and throwing off dire wolf and ice bear alike. I saw that the bear was attached to a large ornate sleigh, and Annaquin placed a powerful foot on the curl of one of the runners and thrust the whole thing forward through the snow, dragging the yelping ice bear with it.

"She's strong," Arthur said, and the rest of us agreed silently.

"Come, dog, bring your pack. No time to dawdle," Annaquin shouted, and we followed dutifully. The Winter's Crystal seemed to have only one gate, right at the base of the castle beneath the tallest of all the ice towers. We weren't far from it, but our path was completely clogged with sleds and sleighs. Ice bears, tall elk, and enormous silver-horned stags were everywhere. "What in the Mothers' names is going on here?" Annaquin said, smacking another aggressive ice bear in the face and ushering us around a group of antsy reindeer.

"These sleighs are piled high with gifts," Merlin said, pointing to the treasures gathered around us.

"Is it a birthday party?" Arthur ventured. "Do the Fae people have birthdays?"

"I think after a few thousand years, I'd stop expecting presents at mine," Morgana said. "How could anyone afford it?"

"No, something far greater is happening," Merlin said. His tone worried me.

"What's going on?" I asked Annaquin, but she pretended she didn't hear me.

"Hey, you there! What are you doing?" a long skinny Fae with drooping ears and a pointy face called to Annaquin. He lowered his blue-diamond-tipped spear, and it glowed with violet light. "You're not allowed in the Winter's Crystal. You've been banished."

"I *am* allowed, you stupid sod," Annaquin growled at him. "Nivian forgave me for all. I banished myself to the Winter Woods." Morgana and I traded a look: *What is that about?* "And I hereby unbanish myself." She took hold of his blue-diamond spearhead with her bare hand and crushed it to sparkling dust.

"Wow!" I said, unable to keep the word in my mouth.

"Now, where's Lady Mithriel? I need to find her. And what's all this nonsense with the gifts and sleighs? Is she having another insipid festival?"

"It is *Queen* Mithriel that you seek," the guardsman answered bitterly. His magic stone was melting into a puddle of silvery water on the ice beneath his feet. He edged away from it. "And this is no mere celebration. It is her coronation. Have you not heard that Lady Nivian is dead? All her great works have melted and cracked. The mortal world has killed her somehow, just as *Queen* Mithriel always said it would."

"*What?*" Annaquin growled, and shoved him against the glittery stone frame of the gate. "You *know* she's dead and you celebrate?"

"Brief mourning services were observed," he choked out. "Tasteful. But the realm must be ruled, and Mithriel is the heir to the—"

"Enough!" Annaquin flung him so hard that the Fae guard sailed over my head. "No one thinks of rescue? Revival? Only a dog and a fire bringer?" The great Fae woman looked at us in fury, and I was frightened for a moment, thinking she'd turn her incredible powers on me.

"I thought of saving her too—" Arthur said, pointing his finger in the air. Morgana clapped a hand over his mouth.

"Quickly, to Mithriel," Annaquin commanded us, ignoring Arthur. "To tell them of your hope! Shame to those who play music and give gifts at the death of our queen, Nivian!"

We reached the great hall in the center of the castle, and for some moments I felt blinded by all that I saw. Sparkling, glowing, golden, and silver shapes undulated and jostled together. It took lots of squinting to identify them. The ceiling rose high into the sky above us and broke apart into three soaring towers. Blue light cast down from the icy glass windows and reflected off silver chandeliers and glistening tile. Before us were throngs of Fae people; creatures made of ice, earth, and fire; shadow beasts; colossal hairy giants; and tiny half-men who gathered at the dirty feet of trolls. These strange beings were numbered in the hundreds and mixed into three columns of crowds before us. The smell of the room was an unsortable tangle.

At the opposite side of the long hall stood a tall Fae woman whose bright, glowing skin made her visible even at a great distance. *There is something special about her,* I thought. I could see the almond shape of her eyes. Less distinct Fae gathered all around her on sunken steps and a raised dais. They were singing an unearthly music that made my ears buzz and twitch, and a bright golden crown was slowly descending toward the woman's head.

"They're crowning her now! We've got to stop this!" Annaquin said, and scooped me up bodily. She charged down the aisle, ignoring Merlin's and Morgana's protests. The sea of monstrous creatures gathered in the great hall went by in a blur. Next I realized, we were on the platform at the front of the hall; Annaquin had knocked over a pair of Fae on the lower steps, and the singing choir above us had gone silent. "Stop the coronation! The queen of Winter can be saved!"

The tall, glowing woman with the almond eyes looked down on us disapprovingly. The scent on her was amazing, as if a hundred human women had the most wonderful parts of their scent signatures all mixed up together. Her eyes pierced me, and like Lady Nivian had done on the lake when I first met her, I felt Lady Mithriel reading my mind.

"You have plans to revive my cousin?" she asked in a voice that was powerful but distant.

"I—I do," I said. "Nivian helped me more than once."

"I know," Lady Mithriel said, her eyes cutting me to the quick. "I can see it plain upon your face. Many loved her. She helped even more. Annaquin, too, you who betrayed her. She restored you, though you could not accept her forgiveness. Is that why you come to me with hopeless plans for her life? Do you wish to be worthy again of her graces?"

"Wha—? Hopeless?" For once, Annaquin looked like she was struggling for words. Shocked Fae peered at us from the sunken steps, and angry Fae glared down from the raised dais. They looked ready to attack us, but Lady Mithriel raised a hand to them.

"There's a magic grail!" I blurted out. "It will bring her back to life. It's in a place called Camelot. I—I'm not sure where. Merlin knows better than me."

Behind me, Arthur and Morgana were helping Merlin hobble up the long, glittering aisle. They tried not to look at the frightening Fae and monsters surrounding them.

Arthur's face was pale, but Morgana seemed determined. Merlin approached in a whirlwind of billowing robes and long white hair.

"My older cousin's human pet," the woman towering above me said. "Merlin, it's been many a year."

"Lady Mithriel," Merlin said, panting with effort. He bowed low, and I heard his spine crackle. "Ten years ago, I was wizard to King Uther Pendragon, the king of men. He loved his people and treated them well, but his wife— Igraine—became deathly ill, and no medicine nor magic could save her. The king called out to the Fae world for help, and Mab answered."

"Our sovereign of dreams. I know this story, humble Merlin. Mab stole the Grail of Life from its rightful place and brought it over to the mortal plane. But the Grail will always return to its home. So Mab advised King Uther to bind the Grail to Camelot, with his wizard's help, I've no doubt—"

"That isn't true!" Merlin interjected. "I railed against it. He exiled me! I warned him what could happen!"

"And so, when the Grail returned to our world, as it always would, it brought the castle, lands, and people of Camelot with it. And Mab has used the dreams of all those mortal minds to wreak havoc ever since!"

"And that—that—" Merlin stammered. Glowing Fae eyes were all around us. At our backs, the mass of unidentifiable monsters stirred and complained. "And that is why our plan must succeed! Help us locate Camelot. There we will find the Grail. I can sever the bond Uther made between the Grail and his castle, and all will be well. Camelot and its people will return to the mortal world and your realm will be rid of them! The Grail waters will revive Nivian. . . ." Merlin turned to the crowd of celebrants behind us and threw open his arms. "Your true queen of Winter will return to you! Lady Mithriel, I beg you. Help us!"

"You shall call me Queen Mithriel now," the sparkling Fae woman said, and reached for the floating crown. She pulled it tight around the soft flowing hair at the top of her head.

"The queen is crowned!" cried a thick-throated Fae at the end of the dais. Powerful voices sang, and the crowd cheered.

"No!" Annaquin said, and grabbed at the crown.

"She assaults the queen!" a thin-armed Fae man shouted. A throng of Winterguards leapt on top of Annaquin and tried to subdue her. A great blast of blue magic sent every one of them flying across the hall. Annaquin raged.

"Leave her, Edbur." Mithriel raised a hand to the thin blue Fae. He crossed his silver spear before his chest, and some forty armed Fae surrounded the throne, ready to strike. "Annaquin, you act without thought—something that has caused you much trouble before. I must be queen if I should help you." Annaquin winced, and Mithriel adjusted the crown. "Mab is sovereign of dreams, and with the mortals of Camelot in her thrall, her powers are greater than ever. I've heard tell she can now control the minds of dragons and even other Fae."

"Just show us the way," Merlin offered humbly. "We will take all the risk. Lead us to Camelot, and if we manage to find the Grail, help spirit us back to Nivian. She died on Avalon—we can show you where."

"Of course it was there," Mithriel huffed. She stroked the crown on her head. "I told my cousin her love for the Otherworld would kill her."

"But *this* is the Otherworld," I said, confused.

Queen Mithriel regarded me coldly. "Maybe by your puny reckoning. By mine, this is the real world, where things matter and last. Magic lives here, and lifewaters flow from golden grails that can raise you from the dead. Your world is the *other* one. Where everything perishes and rots." Morgana put her hand on my back. It was shaking. "I often advised my cousin to break the bridge that connects your dying world to ours. Our magic seeps through and powers petty wizards like yourselves at our expense. And mortal weakness comes the other way, contaminating our precious lands as Mab has done with her dreamers. Now great Nivian has perished there."

"I'm sorry!" I shouted. "It's my fault. I didn't tell her about the worms. But we can save her. Just help us find the Grail. Please!"

Arthur and Morgana were too awed to speak, but they gathered themselves beside me and looked up at the new queen of Winter. Mithriel nodded to the thin blue Fae man. "Edbur, take them to cells where they can rest. Annaquin, join the crowd of celebrants—"

"But, my lady—"

"Your *queen*," Mithriel snapped harshly. "My coronation must be celebrated, and I do not want my hall contaminated with mortal rot. They will wait until we're done, and then we will send a force with them to find the Grail and restore my cousin.

"But—"

"No, do not respond. I command your silence and the mortals' departure." She lifted a long-fingered hand, and Annaquin was thrust back into the crowd of monsters, shadows, and Fae. Blue hands swept us up and turned us away from the queen. The Fae guards' feet were as swift as Annaquin's. I tried to look back over my shoulder at the coronation, but the throne room was already behind us. Merlin, Morgana, and Arthur were bouncing blurs that smeared against the icy hall racing by me. Shouts and cries were the last I heard from them before I found myself thrown down on a sparkling gray floor. My knees wrenched the wrong way, and I yipped. As I turned, a door swung shut and enveloped me in darkness.

I lunged at the heavy door and bit at the icy, frosted skin on the wood. A hard, crackling sound like freezing rock rumbled through the door, and I dropped to the floor. I barked and scratched at the flaky ice.

My Certainty formed, and I blasted the door with fire and shock. The chamber filled with light, and slush turned to steam. But the door stayed shut and everything remained dark.

Somehow, I began to doubt that Queen Mithriel really meant to help.

7

Shattering the Crystal

BANG!

A loud sound woke me. My eyes opened, but my room was still pitch-black.

Bang!

The sound made me leap to my feet. I sniffed the stale air: ice crystals, candle wax, and *wolves*.

Bang!

The door burst open, and my room flooded with torch-light from the hall. My eyes hurt, and I blinked hard. There was a squat silhouette in the doorway.

"Come, boy. It's time to go!"

"Annaquin!" I shouted.

"Nosewise! Good to see you!" Annaquin cuffed my neck and scratched my head. "Yaagh!"

A cold blast of light exploded against her shoulder. I turned on the icy stones and faced down her attacker. It was the pale-blue Fae man who attended Lady Mithriel.

He looked alarmed, but held his hands together like he was praying. Bright light shone from between his fingers, and I realized he was preparing another attack. I dropped into my Mind's Nose and summoned the scent of fire.

"No!" Annaquin shouted, and swept me into the wall with her hefty leg. My face crunched against the gray stones, and fierce magic lit up the hall. I scrambled away and re-readied my spell of fire for the Fae man. But he'd become a snowy ice statue. Through the blurry crystal I could see the magic light dimming in his hands.

"That'll keep him a bit," Annaquin said. She was on the floor behind me and pushed herself up with one hand.

"That's strong magic!" I said, amazed.

"Lady Mithriel has stronger Fae than him," Annaquin said. "And she has no intention of letting you find the Grail."

"But why?" I said. "Nivian is her cousin!"

"She values queenhood more than poor Nivian's life."

"What's going on?" a small voice echoed down the hallway.

"Who's that?" Annaquin asked, her ears twitching.

"Annaquin?" A little girl peeked out from behind the frozen Fae man. Her silky hair draped across her crinkled face. "What did you do to Edbur?"

"Little Liarda, I must take this pup and his friends away," Annaquin said. "Edbur wanted them to stay."

"But why? They're going to help Nivian!" the girl said.

"They are, but they can't do it here," Annaquin responded. "There are folk in the castle who don't want Nivian helped. They want things to stay the way they are."

"Edbur!" The little girl turned and admonished him. "I'm going to tell Mother on you! She's dancing in the Moonhall," Liarda said to Annaquin. "She told me I had to go to bed. But we should tell on Edbur."

"We will tell your mother," Annaquin said to Liarda. She turned her head to me and mouthed, *Lady Mithriel.* "But Nosewise is scared—will you pet him a moment while I get his friends?"

Annaquin poked me in the ribs, and I dropped my ears and tail. "I'm really nervous," I said, shaking slightly. It was the absolute truth.

"Oh, puppy, I'm sorry!" Liarda cooed and ambled over to me, arms outstretched. She caught me in a tight hug and squeezed her face into my fur. She was small. If she were human, I might have guessed she was five years old. But she was a Fae, so she could have been five hundred. Either way, she seemed innocent.

How could Lady Mithriel not want us to save Nivian? Was being the queen of this stupid ice castle really worth it?

Bang! Bang! Bang! Annaquin was assaulting a door down the hall, and I startled at the sound.

"There, there, puppy. Annaquin's going to help!"

I licked her chin and she smiled. Liarda looked more like Nivian than like her mother, Mithriel.

A door burst open, and Arthur swung from the room, draped over Annaquin's shoulder.

"I was asleep!" Arthur complained, and Annaquin dropped him to the floor and tossed Excalibur alongside him. He pressed his fists into his eyes, and I ran to him.

"Puppy!" Liarda called behind me.

"Arthur," I said. "Are you all right?"

"I was fine," he said, tugging at the corners of his eyes. "Until a wild Fae woman dragged me out of bed."

"She's rescuing us!"

"I can see that," Arthur said, blinking his eyes wide open. Annaquin knocked down another two doors, and Morgana and Merlin each appeared from their rooms, much more awake and alert than Arthur.

"Nosewise!" Morgana said, running over.

"She means to keep the crown for herself!" Merlin shouted. "Mithriel loves power more than her own kin—"

"Man Wizard!" Annaquin gestured to Liarda.

Merlin put a hand over his mouth, embarrassed.

"What did he say about Mommy?" Liarda asked me. "We need to tell her Edbur tried to hurt you."

"Wait," Morgana said, immediately catching on to the

situation. "You should go to bed. We'll tell your mother about Edbur."

"I can do it!" Liarda answered.

"Just stay with us," Annaquin said. "See us out of the castle."

"I'm old enough to walk the halls myself!"

"Hold on a minute," Morgana said, gently grabbing her wrist.

Liarda's forearm skin glowed and thickened into icy crystal. Morgana shrieked and withdrew her hand. "I'll be right back!" Liarda called, and disappeared, skipping down the hall.

Merlin hesitantly leveled his Asteria in her direction, but Annaquin slapped it away. "We haven't time."

The five of us tore through the icy halls wordlessly but not soundlessly. Arthur kept clanging Excalibur against the floor, and even in its wool scabbard it chimed like a bell. Morgana whimpered as she ran. And Annaquin had thrown Merlin over her shoulder, and he grunted with her every step.

We all spilled into an indoor garden. Lush green trees thrived in pots, and spiky vines climbed iron grates affixed to the wall. Their wide leaves opened to an enormous glass window that curved up to form both wall and ceiling. I pressed my nose to it and beheld the starry sky.

Crash! Annaquin shattered the ice panes, and shards fell away from us. I poked my head out and saw a steep drop of maybe forty feet. The ice disappeared into the distant snow.

"Go on! Jump!" Annaquin shouted, knocking out the last of the ice glass.

"Are you crazy?" Arthur gaped at her.

"Fly if you'd rather!" she said, then grabbed him by his shirt and tossed him out the window.

"Hey!" Morgana shouted, and bent over the ledge with me to watch him fall. He landed with a crunch, and puffs of snow dust kicked up around him.

"Did it hurt?" Annaquin called in her thick brogue.

"Just my whole body," Arthur groaned from below.

"He's exaggerating. Fly or jump?"

"Jump," Morgana said quickly, and I echoed her. Hopefully I could land on my feet.

"Just don't fall on him—you'll be fine!"

"Ready, boy?" Morgana said.

I yipped and leapt over the edge. The wind and the snow blinded me, and my mane whipped all around my face. My stomach felt loose and sick. Something slapped the bottom of my jaw and crunched against my legs, and I was in the snow.

"Ouch," I said, wrenching my head free of the snow that engulfed it. I was half buried.

Morgana was stuck beside me, and we watched wordlessly as Merlin was hurled out the window. His robes caught the air and puffed like wings spread across his bony body. He looked like a bat that had forgotten how to fly.

Annaquin came down after him.

She was good on the snowpack. She attached netted wooden shoes to the bottoms of her feet and stomped on top of the snow without falling through. One by one she came and lifted us. Merlin went on her shoulder again; Morgana and Arthur were each tucked under an arm. Then she plucked me out of the Nosewise-shaped hole in the snow.

"You're the only one with the feet for this," she said as she gently set me down. To my amazement, my toe pads spread and I could walk across the snow without falling through. Four legs really were better than two!

We quickly trudged to a stand of pines hidden in the shadow of the Winter's Crystal, and Annaquin lifted a big, low branch.

I'd known I'd smelled wolves! The whole dire-wolf pack was waiting there. Felan proudly held his spot at the front, while the rest stood ready in their collars. Tails started wagging when the wolves saw Annaquin, and they howled and yipped. Felan snarled, silencing the pack.

Annaquin dumped Merlin, Arthur, and Morgana on the back of the sled. I jumped aboard, and she took up the reins before me. The leathers were in her hand; she rose them to crack—

Crack! The great pine tree that had hidden the sled wolves from the castle burst at the trunk. It groaned and crashed into the snow, revealing a small army of Fae sleighs, pulled by elk and ice bears, rounding the castle and charging toward us, flush with magic.

"Felan, sic!" Annaquin called, and dropped the reins. The black dire wolf shook off his collar and bolted over the felled pine toward the Fae. Annaquin followed, her hands charging up with magic of her own. "Nosewise to the front! Take the sled through the forest!"

"What?" I shouted. "Where?"

"Far as it goes!" she said, launching herself over the tree and unleashing a storm of Winter sorcery.

I looked to Merlin.

"As she says, boy!"

"Nosewise, go!" Morgana encouraged me.

I leapt off the sleigh and saw Arthur out of the corner of my eye. He held Excalibur limply.

We couldn't fight them. We needed to run. And with Felan gone, I had to lead the sled.

I tried not to be too happy about it.

The lead collar was at the front, right between the two lines of dire wolves. They were all taller than me, bigger and stronger. But I was the one at the head of the pack.

Felan's collar dwarfed my chest and shoulders, but no one laughed this time. I tugged against the leather, barked loud and strong like Felan did, and we were off.

These wolves were fast, and they loved to run. I could hear it in their short pants and springy steps. I love running too, but they were twice as tall as me and they were used to racing through the snow. I was falling behind the front two wolves of each line, and our ropes were tangling.

So I cheated. But only out of necessity.

Blast! I sent a burst of wind and shock down at the snow beneath my feet, and the force thrust me up and forward. My ankles rattled, but for a brief second I flew. My paws landed in the snow, and I did it again.

Puff! I refined it a little and got enough force to lift and propel me, but not to blast my legs apart.

It was working. With each burst of magic I gained ground. The female to my left graciously leaned to the side and let me pass, but the gray to my right snarled at me. The little explosions of magic were spooking him.

Someone was shouting behind me, but wind, mushing wolves, and magic were drowning out the sound. I craned my neck and spotted Merlin waving his arms. The distraction sent me back so far that the two dire wolves at the front were practically dragging me.

Puff! Puff! Puff!

I tried more magic to get me in formation. But the gray

male was struggling with the rope and turning our sled outward to the right. The high snow protected it from any gnarly roots or fallen logs that could trip us, but the woods were full of thick tree trunks that we needed to avoid.

And I had no idea where we were supposed to be going. Annaquin had only said to take the sled through the forest "as far as it goes," but what did that mean? The sled was shifting and curving according to the gray male's fancy. The other wolves were unhappy; I saw them tugging against the direction of the lines.

Scree! A sparkling beam of light shot over my head and wound its way through the snowy trees to my left. Merlin was showing me where to go! Some wolves raised their heads to watch, but the gray male ignored it and turned everyone from the path.

Everyone but me.

Blast! I sent a tremendous shock at the snow beneath my feet. My knuckles bruised, but I flew to the side of the errant gray wolf.

Puff! Puff! Puff! My Asteria got me cheek to cheek with him, and he nipped at me. I winced away from his sharp teeth and dropped behind him.

Puff! Puff! Puff! I built up my speed, and he snarled and lunged again.

I was ready this time. When his snout came at me, I filled his nose with a gust of wind.

"Yip!" he cried, and turned, shaking his head. Dogs hate someone blowing in their nose. It makes them feel disjointed and funny. So never do it unless you need to overtake a dire-wolf pack. That's the only time it's okay.

The lines straightened behind me. Merlin sent another beam of sparkling light through the trees to guide me, and—*Puff! Puff! Puff!*—I turned the pack in that direction.

Merlin's light showed the way through the forest, and I would take us as far as it went.

PART III

8

The Great Dreaming

THE WOLVES CAME TO A DEAD STOP. IT WAS VERY SUDDEN. WE'D been running along at a fast clip, and I'd been focused on keeping up with my magic, when the whooping wolves went silent and the sled skidded to a standstill.

"Come on!" I commanded the wolves, and tugged them ahead. I barked my most authoritative woof. The white, gray, and black wolves looked nervous, some sitting and others lying down in resignation.

Behind them I saw Merlin ushering Morgana and Arthur from the sled. All three immediately sank into the deep snow. "It's easier with four legs!" I said, ducking out of my collar and loping up to them.

"Just help me through this bit," Merlin said, struggling as Arthur and Morgana pulled him through the snow. "It gets better over there."

The pine forest ended and one made up of maple and ash stretched before us. There was no snow in the trees ahead, no snow on the forest floor either. Big, gnarled roots crowded between the tree trunks.

"Where are we?" Morgana asked.

I turned to Merlin. He'd set the path.

"I believe this is the outer edge of the Winter Lands," Merlin said. "The wolves refuse to go any further."

"Will we be safe over there?" Morgana asked.

"Safe from some things, endangered by others."

"It looks warm," Arthur said. "What is it?"

"Haven't the faintest idea," Merlin answered with a weary laugh.

Morgana and Arthur supported Merlin as we trudged through the snow, but with every step it grew shallower. Soon there was only slush beneath my feet.

"If you don't know where we are, then why'd you lead me here?" I asked Merlin.

"I didn't lead you here," Merlin answered. "I led you away from there. I can read the Fae sky fairly well. And I just sent you in the opposite direction of the Winter's Crystal."

"Haven't you been to the Fae realm before?" I asked, impatient with his explanation.

"Yes, once," Merlin answered. "With you, Nosewise. When we were all prisoners of Oberon."

"That's the only time?"

"Haven't you known the Lady for years?" asked Arthur.

Morgana shook her head. "You two don't realize what a strange experience we've had."

"Very unique," Merlin agreed. He shook his robes free of snow. "Mortals visit the Fae realm in their dreams, it is said, and also when they die. To be both awake and alive in the Otherworld is quite rare."

"And to get out—" Morgana added.

"Never," Merlin said.

"That's what I was telling you, Nosewise," Arthur said. "When we first found the faerie ring. I said folks that go in never come out."

"But we did!" I said.

"Maybe a singular experience in the history of mortals and the Fae," Merlin said emphatically. "I've known Lady Nivian for sixty years and was never once invited on a tour. And I didn't want to go. This is a land of the dead, of the dreaming, of mysteries! Dire wolves! Ice castles! Courts of Fae plotting against each other. We have no place here!"

Merlin smiled at us. The absurdity of it all was making him loopy. "I'm glad you thought it was such a casual thing, Nosewise, to cross over into the Otherworld. Or else we might have missed our chance, and Nivian would be bereft of hope. Speaking of that—*fweet!*" Merlin whistled through his teeth and waved his hand at the pack of dire wolves. "Back to your mistress now! She needs you!"

The wolves' ears perked, but they stayed still.

"Do you think Annaquin is . . ." Morgana stopped herself short.

"She can hold her own; I've no doubt about that," Merlin said. "But she may be captured. She'll need her wolves for when she escapes. Go on now!"

The wolves didn't move, but some of them looked at me. My tail wagged wildly.

"So proud of himself," Morgana said, patting my head.

"All right, boy," said Merlin. "You dismiss them."

I popped out my chest and sauntered over to my pack. "Dire wolves," I said in my deepest, gruffest voice, "you've been great companions. We ran over the snow together and we pulled a heavy sled. There was lots of stuff to stop and sniff, but we kept on running. Good job, pack! Now back to Annaquin!"

I flicked my ears and my Asteria glowed bright. The wolves looked at me with rapt attention, but they were still.

"You need to talk dog to them!" Morgana reminded me.

Oh, right! I gave them three short barks and pointed back toward the castle. The wolves leapt up and joyfully chugged the sled in a wide circle, barking their goodbyes to us. In a moment they were running out of sight.

"Well, that's done," Merlin said, walking over to me and patting my back. He wheeled about on his heels, taking in the forest behind us. "Now we just need to figure where in the Otherworld we are."

It was darker in these parts of the woods, with no bright snow to reflect the starlight. Merlin hesitated to use Asteria light until we knew where we were. Navigating the dark wasn't a problem for me; I could hear my footfalls echo against the tree roots. And my whiskers kept me informed of anything directly before me. My human companions were not so fortunate.

"Oh! Ow!" Arthur cried, tripping over a root. He huddled on the forest floor and hugged his knees.

"Are you hurt?" Morgana asked.

Arthur shook his head. He looked distraught. "I feel hopeless," he sighed. "We won't find the Grail out here! We won't even survive!" Hot tears streamed down his cheeks as he sobbed.

"Arthur?" I asked, pressing up to him. Merlin and Morgana were stumbling to get near us. Arthur cried wretchedly, coughing and snotting on himself. I'd never known him to despair like this. I licked his face and neck, trying to comfort him.

Then he stopped.

"Uh, sorry. I don't know what that was," he said, standing up. "What just happened to me?"

"Arthur," Merlin said cautiously, "if you need us to stop and rest . . ."

"No, I don't. Something came over me. Like a hundred-pound weight on my chest. Then it was gone."

"When did it start?" Morgana asked in the dark.

"When I tripped on that tree root." Arthur pointed to an old knotty maple.

"This one?"

"Careful, child!" Merlin shouted as Morgana laid her hand on a branch.

"I've done something wrong!" Morgana cried, and dropped to the ground and curled into a ball. "So stupid! Now I feel awful!"

That tree is making them crazy.

"Saturated with emotion . . . ," Merlin said ponderously. "I think I have some idea of where we are."

"What does it matter?" Morgana said wretchedly. "We're never going to find Camelot."

"She's under a sadness spell," I said.

"Not everything is a spell," Merlin answered. "What counts for magic in our world is in this place simply nature."

An orange light swept through the trees and cast deep shadows across Merlin's robes. Morgana stopped crying and looked up. "What was that?"

I turned and saw a rush of foggy light slither off into the woods and leave us in darkness again.

"It's not a safe place, but near to our destination," Merlin said, finally letting his Asteria glow with light. "You must work to keep your minds clear. There are forces that—"

"Here comes another one," Arthur interrupted.

A small gray-yellow cloud filtered through the trees and blew toward us.

"Think of nothing!" Merlin's voice was swallowed by the light.

The freshly kneaded loaves plopped onto my iron tray one by one. My hands were coated in fine, sweet-smelling flour. Each doughy loaf left globs between my fingers as I tried to set them on the tray. Soon the dough was coating my arms and face.

The oven was far away, all the way across the bakery. Voices murmured in some unseen room. They belonged to my wife and daughter, calling out for bread. I tried to answer them, but my mouth was stuffed with dough.

The oven was impossibly far away. The dough and the dull heat thickened the air so much that I couldn't breathe. I grabbed at my throat, the flour dust—

Cold light cut through the dust and the bakery disappeared. I found myself in a dark forest with Merlin, Arthur, and Morgana. Merlin's Asteria pressed against my forehead. With a flick of the wrist, he drew it away.

"I was in a bakery?" I said.

"These are the Dreamlands," Merlin answered stiffly. "Queen Mab's domain."

"Queen Mab," Morgana said, helping Arthur back to his feet. "Does that mean we're close?"

"Yes. Camelot should be near, but we must keep our wits about us."

"I was in a bakery?" I said, still bewildered. "Why did I have hands?"

"I was there too!" Arthur said. "The dough was choking me!"

"That cloudy apparition caught you both as it slithered by," Merlin said. "It may sound strange, but that was someone's dream."

"What? Whose dream?" I asked.

"A baker's, perhaps," Merlin answered. "The Otherworld and our mortal one are closely connected. When we dream, our minds descend from our world into this one. They wander the woods, intermingle, and return when their dreamers wake. That is why prophecy may be found in dreams."

"And why they're weird," Arthur said. "They live in a spooky wood."

"I'll never fall asleep again," Morgana said, watching a ghastly cloud of light screech by.

"It's safe to have a dream," Merlin said. "But wandering the Dreamlands is another story—*ack!* Morgana!"

A finger of mist slid up Morgana's spine and entered the back of her head. "The blueberries are having their dance tonight!" she shrieked, and skipped away from us, flailing her arms. "How un-berry-like of them not to invite you! What a breach of protocol!"

She landed clumsily and crashed to the forest floor. "Unsanitary!" she shouted.

Merlin, Arthur, and I raced to her, and Merlin pressed the Asteria to her forehead. "Out! Out!" He reared back his staff, and green light spilled from Morgana's head. He shooed it away with the stone, and the green dream slithered into the woods.

"Oh! Uh!" Morgana groaned. "I don't like this!" She put a hand on my shoulder and pressed herself to her feet.

"How did you do that?" I asked Merlin.

"A dispel," he said, raising his staff. "Not simple magic."

"I wish we had more time to—*hyah!*" Merlin sent a blast of bright magic at an incoming dream. He knocked it off course, and the dream wormed between the trees.

"They look like they're coming for us," I said.

"They may be," Merlin answered. "Or just darting about. Dreams are a mystery."

"Can this help?" Arthur asked, removing Excalibur from its sheath. The sword glowed in the darkness and brightened Arthur's face. His lips were pulled tight and his eyelids twitched.

"Cut at dreams with the sword?" Merlin said warily. "I'm sure I don't know. It couldn't hurt!"

"Behind the tree!" Morgana pointed over Arthur's shoulder.

He spun into a hazy cloud of light and swung Excalibur up from the ground, splitting the dream in half. The lights in the cloud died out, and the smoky mass sank to the ground.

"So I just cut someone's brain in two?" Arthur asked, horrified.

"You're worried about them?" Merlin asked. "Perhaps their dream came to a shocking end, they woke up, and they went for a sip of water. Look where we are!" Merlin held out his hands. More lights were slipping through the trees around us. The dreams were truly everywhere. "Let's move. Keep close. Stay vigilant."

The four of us slowly made our way through the woods, careful to avoid emotion-soaked trees and rogue dreams. Every few steps Merlin had to knock back an approaching dream, and Arthur swung at them with his sword. But there were too many in the woods.

"Morgana, do you know how to dispel?" I asked, taking her sleeve in my mouth.

"What? I think," she answered, her eyes flitting between the dreams Arthur and Merlin were battling. "To cast a dispel you must be able to imagine a person's mind. You must see what's true and cast all else away."

"Take my Asteria, then. They need your help."

"I'm not sure I can—and your voice."

"You can give it back; just take it for now. Until Camelot."

Morgana's face twisted guiltily. Merlin still wouldn't let her have an Asteria of her own because of what she'd done to aid Oberon.

"Morgana," I said, pawing my neck.

"All right. All right," she answered, crouching and taking hold of my collar. "Just for now, until we're safe from the rabbits."

My ears twitched.

"What?" I said.

"The bunnies here. They want to dance with our garden vegetables. But we've got a cure for it." She leaned down and whispered in my ear, "The spanking cure."

A faint yellow dream was pouring into her mind from a tree branch. She let go of my collar and sprang up.

"Rabbits!" she shouted madly. "Rabbits!"

"Morgana's caught a dream!" I said. "Merlin, she needs you!"

His back was to me, and he was swiping at something with his staff. Blue and yellow dreams slipped by him. I ran up to his knee. He found my head with his hand and looked down at me with a mad expression. "That's why I'm the pawnbroker and you're just a chamber pot!"

He was dreaming.

115

"Wake up!" I shouted. "Dispel! Dispel!" I shook the Asteria on my neck in a vain attempt to get it to do *something*. Why did magic have to be so hard?

I turned to Arthur. Excalibur could be dangerous, but I'd seen it dispel a dream. Maybe if he was gentle, he could get Merlin—

"Flattery!" Arthur was cooing. He casually swung Excalibur through the air.

"Arthur!" I called to him, cautiously stepping around the dreams that floated in my path. A green dream like a fly swarm buzzed toward my head, and I leapt away to dodge it.

"Arthur!" I shouted, getting as close as I could. "Wake up!"

He stopped flailing the sword and turned to me. His eyes blinked, but they were looking in different directions.

"Just stay still," I said. He was far gone, but if I could take the hilt in my mouth I could drag Excalibur to Merlin. Maybe brushing it against him would be enough to dispel the dream.

Arthur stood stock-still, staring blankly at some unknown sight behind me. His mind was gone, but his body was resting. I stretched my neck until I was within an inch of his sword-wielding hand. Gently, so as not to disturb him, I set my teeth on Excalibur's cross guard and readied myself to yank. This would be pulling the sword from the stone all over again.

"Flibert," Arthur said in a friendly voice.

116

The nonsense word shocked me so much that I released the sword, perked my ears, and said, "What?"

"Flibert!" Arthur repeated triumphantly, and hoisted Excalibur above his head with two hands. He turned and ran at top speed into the ghostly forest.

"Wait!" I shouted, running after him.

But the other horses in the barn were making a terrible racket.

They neighed and rattled in their stalls so much that I couldn't stand it. I kicked my door and found myself outside, galloping happily across the open pasture.

The wolf pack was in a frenzy. The nine of us gathered around the felled deer. The big gray went first. He was the alpha of our pack, and I was afraid of him. He was my brother. Our mother had died before we were done nursing. Our aunt had raised us until we learned to hunt.

When the old alpha died, the two of us fought, and he won.

I scampered into the barn and saw the mountain of grain. I shoved pawfuls of oats into my whiskered mouth. Pleasure filled me from toes to tail.

An alarm scent hit my nose and I bolted. The grain spilled from my mouth and scattered on the floor. The scratch of claws against wood filled my ears. An enormous hairy monster, a cat, careened toward my chest, mouth agape—fangs bared.

The dream state lifted like a heavy wool blanket. I was cold and in the middle of a vast clearing. The woods were gone. Only dry, crackling grass was beneath me. I shook myself, and the hair stood up on my neck.

Dreams swirled all around me like ghosts. Some were loud and others seemed to sparkle as they floated by. Somehow they made more sense to me now. This one was a rabbit's dream of his time in the den. That other one was a young girl arguing with her mother. At a glance I knew the basic shape of each. There were wolf, cat, sheep, horse, mouse, and human dreams all swirling together through the endless field.

Some seemed determined to avoid one another, while others crossed paths, mingled, and departed changed. It was scary to be in the middle of all these dreams.

I slowly spun around, looking for my pack. But Arthur, Merlin, and Morgana were nowhere to be seen. I panicked. How long had I been dreaming? Had we wandered away from one another? I sniffed the Fae realm air but found no trace of them.

Slowly I crept across the dying grass. My mouth was dry, and I feared that each of us would starve on our feet, sleep-walking.

There was a clacking to my right, and I turned just in time to see an old man's dream lumbering toward me.

My knees were nimble like they hadn't been in years, and I skipped across the field behind our ancestral home, playing a game of wheel and stick with my grandson.

"Are you awake?" asked a woman with an impatient voice. Her eyes looked down on me like two stars. Her wide face shone dully, like a wet stone.

She leaned over me with her arms outstretched. Long drapes of fabric hung from her hands and shoulders, embroidered with endless scenes from stories. There were lions fighting in pits, and humans reaping grain and making war. Great flocks of birds stitched from golden thread flew from one arm of her robe to the other. Everything moved, animals and men tumbling over each other in the stitching. I tried to follow the stories, but they dropped out of sight, and her enormous moon face was all I could see, her pointed nose making contact with my own.

"You are awake!" she said in a thrilling voice. "You must tell me who you are!"

"Nosewise," I said. "A dog."

"Yes," she said rapturously, and spun a dozen scenes of nature across her robes. "A dog who speaks! I heard you as you walked within my dreams. Tell me now," she said, fluffing the fabric of her robe into a kind of tent that covered our heads, "how did you come to be?"

The strange woman enveloped me in the billowing fabric, and I glanced at the scenes dancing about me. *Who is this woman who claims the dreams? She is powerful and a Fae. She must be Queen Mab, I thought.*

The sight of her frightened me into telling the truth. I didn't want to be lost in a dream again. "I'm a wizard's pet. My master is Merlin; my girl is Morgana. She lent me her Asteria once and it let me talk. I know some magic. Please don't hurt me."

"And I am Queen Mab. Welcome to my woods. You are safe now that I am near. You say Merlin is your master? I know him!" said the queen of dreams. "I found him wandering some days ago!"

"Days ago?" How long had I been dreaming?

"Yes! And two children, too. All lost in dreams!" she laughed. "Hardly remembering their own names, so there was little they could tell me of themselves. But Merlin I recognized!"

"They didn't know themselves?"

"Of all mortals, humans are the most baffled by dreams. They hold fast to stories they tell about themselves in the day; a night story is no different."

I could feel the Fae queen's sweet breath against my nose. She seemed to be drinking me in through her eyes. Even a small lie would have no place to hide.

"Morgana is the girl, and Arthur is the boy," I said. "We all live together with Merlin. He came with us into the Otherworld."

"And so it falls together, the tale," Queen Mab said, lacing together her jeweled fingers. "Why, may I ask, did Merlin bring his mortal friends to this dreaming place?"

There was no room for lies, but some truths didn't have to leave my mouth. "For reasons I don't completely understand," I said. There was no lie in that.

"A puzzle, then, for me to solve." Queen Mab laughed and drew me close. Her scent was a hundred different smells and stories. She was a young sheep, an old wolf, a newborn pup, a sick man, and so on, over many lifetimes and ages. She was powerful and strange and she frightened me.

"My dear dog, this is no place for mortals." With a *crack!* the multicolored robe fell away, and I saw we were surrounded by ghastly dreams. They tried to rush in and take me, but Mab leapt into the sky, lifting me with her.

"Calm yourself, pup!" she said, clamping me tighter. "I have a mortal place where one like you will be safe and free to serve me well!" She cackled and flew low across the dreamscape, dragging me through the hazy air while my toes dipped into the terrifying dreams below.

9

Happy Home Again

THE OTHERWORLD SPED BELOW US LIKE A RUSHING RIVER. HOT air blew past my ears and made them ring. The wind was harsh, and I had to close my eyes.

Then it stopped. I felt my legs dangle beneath Mab's bony grip, and I slowly opened my eyes.

There was an enormous valley below me, curving down for miles. I saw farmland cut into square fields growing crops of different colors. Houses and barns dotted the landscape, and each little chimney spouted smoke. Dirt roads snaked between the fields, and people and animals walked them with their carts.

Farther down there was a dense town center. Hundreds of buildings huddled together, and great plumes of black smoke sent sulfur and charcoal up into the sky. I heard people, too, shouting and talking to each other. There must have been thousands of them.

"That's my prize, little pup," Mab purred in my ear. "Can

you see it from here? Castle Camelot. The jewel at the heart of my kingdom."

She pointed, and I saw the walled-off circle in the center of the town, protecting a fuzzy-looking castle. It was so far away it blended into the rest of the town. *That's where the Grail is supposed to be!*

"And you, my sweet, should play a part in it all," Mab said, swiftly lowering us to the ground. As we fell, I lost sight of the castle in the faraway city. A small farmhouse completely obscured it, but I kept my snout pointing in the right direction. The second Mab let go of me, I planned to charge away and make for Camelot. Lady Nivian was depending on me.

"You're home, Little Nosewise." Queen Mab released me from her grip and set me on the grass. The moment I felt her fingers loosen, I dropped my head and ran.

But something stopped me short, like a blast of magic at the back of my head.

This wasn't just any farmhouse, I realized. It was the place that I called home. I'd been looking for my home all this time, and here it was! Mab had brought me right to it! My heart sighed at the sight of the house with its square door and the big barn set off to the side. I had many happy memories here, though I couldn't think of any in particular.

But that didn't matter now. This was my house. It was where my family lived. I couldn't think of their names, not this instant, nor what they looked like, nor how many there were. But I knew this was my family home.

"Where are they?" I asked Queen Mab, and I was reminded of how much I loved her. She watched over all of us in Camelot. We each owed our life to her, but she never asked for anything in return. Only our loyalty and happiness.

"You want to know where your family is?" Queen Mab asked, looking pleased. I liked when Queen Mab was pleased with me. "They're working the fields. But they ought to be coming now to greet you." She gestured in the direction of wheatgrass, which shifted in the wind. I perked my ears and waited eagerly.

A tall man pushed away the wheat and came bounding out of the field. The moment we laid eyes on each other, we both lit up with joy. My tail wagged uncontrollably, and I leapt across the earth to greet my master. His short beard and bald head instantly comforted me. I'd known this man my entire life.

I set my paws on his chest and licked his face. He laughed and ran his burly hands over my ears.

"Good boy! My dog! I love my good dog!" the man said, smiling.

"Master! I missed you!" My mouth waggled as I tried to speak his name; I felt it was just on the tip of my tongue.

"Reunited again," Queen Mab said, stepping beside us. "Nosewise and his beloved master, Walder Ashdown."

"Walder!" I said, the name ringing true.

"Nosewise," Walder said, gently gripping my ear. *This is the way things are supposed to be,* I thought, *Walder and me. Just the two of us making our way in the world.*

"And here comes the mistress," Queen Mab cooed, and I saw a woman walking down the dirt road over the hill. I recognized her instantly. *My mistress!* I thought, but struggled again with her name.

She waved and dropped the reins of another familiar creature. It was as tall as a horse but had a serpent's head, scaly skin, ridged plates all along its back, and thick legs that ended in long, sharp claws. *I've seen one of those before,* I thought.

The lady came running toward me. She bent down, and I reached up for a kiss.

"Alma, I've returned your dog," Queen Mab cooed again. "Nosewise," she added sharply.

"Nosewise, I've missed you," Alma said. "Where have you been?"

I opened my mouth to answer her, but strangely enough, I couldn't remember. I flattened my ears and looked to Queen Mab.

"You were out chasing squirrels in the forest!" Queen Mab said. She glanced at Alma. "You were worried sick about him."

"We were worried sick about you," Alma said, embracing me. I buried my snout in her long brown hair. I sniffed her familiar scent and started to cry.

"I'll never run away again," I whined. "You and Walder are my only family in the world. Please forgive me."

Alma pulled back and gave me a funny look.

"Not your only family," Queen Mab said tersely. "The girl. Where is she?"

A high-pitched shriek cut through the air, and rows of grain shook as a long, squat beast burst from the field. Its bony elbows jutted out at wide angles, and an enormous underbite sent two long teeth right up past its diamond-shaped eyes. A small pair of wings flailed and helped it skid to a stop in the dust. A young girl with light brown hair rode on its back, holding on to the pair of horns atop its fuzzy head. I reminded myself how very normal it was to see people riding creatures like this.

The young girl leapt down and scrambled through the dust in a panic. She looked afraid and short of breath. But she was part of my family too.

"Queen Mab!" The girl knelt low in the dust and held up her hands to the queen in a gesture of submission. We all loved Queen Mab, very much.

"Rise, Winnie, and look," the Queen said, lifting the girl's chin. "I have returned your dog, Nosewise, to you."

"Winnie, I missed you!" I said, my tail wagging. I went to lick her face, but Winnie winced and pulled away from me. That was a shock; she'd raised me from the time I was a pup.

A fleeting look of dread crossed her face. Then she smiled wide and extended her hands to me. "Nosewise, my puppy," she said stiffly. "I—I'd wondered where you'd been."

"I ran after some squirrels," I told her, not quite as sure as I'd been a moment before. Something in Winnie's face made me doubt myself.

"Oh, boy." She snapped her fingers awkwardly. "You're always doing that. Running away. I guess that's just how dogs are."

"Yes, he needs more training!" Walder said, ruffling the hair on my head. He made me feel better. I could remember all the tricks Walder had taught me to do: Sit! Stay! Speak!

"Don't do that again," Alma scolded me gently. "You gave us a fright!" She scratched my back, and I felt all the joys of family.

"Yes, uh, it's good to have our dog back," Winnie said, sharing a stiff smile between the family and Mab. Winnie made me feel uncomfortable, like I didn't belong here. *Is that why I was chasing squirrels?*

"The family is together again," Mab said, putting her hand on Winnie's shoulder. She eyed the girl with wariness, but only a little. Winnie smiled wide and bright. "The sun's about to set," Queen Mab added, looking up at the sky. "Why don't you enjoy a family dinner?"

"Thanks for bringing Nosewise home!" Walder said.

"We're grateful, our queen," Alma bowed.

"Thank you!" I shouted, my tail wagging. Winnie nodded her head vigorously.

"Everything for my subjects." Queen Mab smiled sharply. She laughed and took to the sky. Our eyes followed her swooping path down the valley toward the city below. I was always thrilled when I had a chance to watch the queen fly, even though I was very used to it.

Walder and Alma waved vigorously and shouted praise at the queen. I wagged my tail and barked. Winnie was standing beside me. With one hand she waved at the queen; the other one she'd buried deep in the fur of my mane, and I noticed it was shaking, violently.

At supper there were no bowls with food and water placed on the floor for me. "I was cleaning them," Alma said, and stood up from the table. She wandered to a shelf in the corner of the main room, where a stack of wooden bowls was kept. She took two and set them on the floor.

"Could I have some water, please?" I asked.

"Of course," Alma answered. She hefted a pail and

poured water into my wooden bowl, splashing it everywhere. I lapped it up eagerly and thought I must have been chasing squirrels a long time, because I was very thirsty.

Winnie, the girl, scooted off her seat and poured the remains of her chunky stew into my food bowl. The meat had a strange taste, but one that I knew well.

"Sorry they're not ready for you," Winnie said. "She's used to making supper for three."

"That's not true," Alma said. "I always make enough for Nosewise."

"No lying about your mother—you're always lying." Walder pointed his spoon at her. He seemed mean.

But I loved him, I remembered. And he wasn't mean. Winnie was just telling a lie. She did that sometimes.

Winnie shrank from her father and rubbed my head. "I'll find something more for you."

Walder's angry eyes followed her across the common room. She disappeared behind a door and emerged with a handful of bright berries. They smelled sharp, and each little drupelet spouted thin hairs. The girl poured the handful of berries into my bowl after I finished the stew.

I took a mouthful and remembered this salty, sweet taste. I'd definitely had these before.

Winnie patted my back and sat at the table with our family.

We finished dinner quietly that night, hardly speaking

and barely moving except for fidgety Winnie. A great calm beset me, and I felt no inclination to do anything.

When I next realized it, the house had become dark. The sun was well below the horizon, and only the faint light gave shape to the people and objects in our home.

"Time for sleeping," Walder said.

"Quite true, my dear," Alma said. The two of them rose and walked to their bedroom, saying good-nights over their shoulders.

I leapt up to follow them into their room—I always slept near my masters—but Winnie stopped me.

"Nosewise, why don't you sleep with me tonight?" I remembered that I often slept with Winnie and wagged my tail happily.

"I'm tired," I said, pressing my nose to her thigh. She stroked my head.

"I know, boy. Come now, let us sleep."

I followed her into a bedroom. Her distinct smell was all around, and I heard her lie down on a straw bed. I leapt up and felt the scratchy straw-and-cloth mattress with my nose.

I plopped down in Winnie's arm and she stroked my head as I fell asleep. The room was so dark, I didn't even need to close my eyes.

❧

"Wake up, Nosewise! Wake up!"

Sharp hands were pressing me and shaking me wildly across the scratchy bed. My legs were flailing, and I bit my tongue.

I yipped and saw a round face, lit by a candlelight.

She was a stranger.

"Stay quiet!" the girl said, pressing my lips. She grabbed my snout and shook my head by the nose. "Are you awake? Are you awake?"

"Yes! Who are you?"

I was in a candlelit bedroom. Everything felt very wrong.

"You don't know who I am? You don't recognize me?" She leaned into me as the candlelight cast dancing shadows across her face.

"You're the girl from my dream. I dreamed about you."

"I'm Winnie," she said. "You *were* dreaming, and you *weren't*."

"What?" I looked around the room. It was the one in the dream, in the little farmhouse. "What do you mean?"

"It's complicated." The girl stood up from the bed. She took the waxy candle off her dresser and used it to light three more.

"Queen Mab did that to you," Winnie said. "She made you dream."

Queen Mab, I remembered, *the Fae*. "I went through lots of dreams," I said. "They came to me in the forest."

"It's not like that here," Winnie said. "I ran away once and got lost in that forest. The dreams caught me again and again, until Queen Mab retrieved me. What she does here is different." Winnie sighed. "You know how, if you're having a dream, weird stuff is likely to happen? Dogs do dream, don't they?"

"I dream."

"And sometimes the dreams are weird, right?"

"My dreams are strange."

"But they seem normal when you're in them, don't they?" Winnie held up her finger. "In a dream, you accept everything."

"I guess." I thought back to all the dreams I'd had at the foot of Merlin's bed.

"She puts us into a dream state here, so that everything seems normal. The dragon beasts all around, a flying Fae woman. She even had Mom and Dad thinking you were our dog. We've never had a dog. Especially not one who talks. When Mab appeared with you, I thought I was back in the dream state myself."

"I thought I lived here," I said. "I was sure of it."

"That's Mab working on you. But I woke you up from it. A good fright can do that."

"Why don't you wake your parents?" I said.

"They'd go mad. I've tried it before. They see the dragons and griffins we're milking on the farm, the lizard people,

the flying witch, and soon they're screaming their heads off, waking up the neighbors. Then Queen Mab swoops down and casts her spell, and it's like it never happened."

"But—then how are you awake?"

"I *hide* it," Winnie said seriously. "Mab's put me down before, and I've slept for ages. You've got to keep it secret or she'll put you under."

"Isn't it scary lying to her?" I thought of the way her eyes bore into me.

"Terrifying," she answered. "It would be easier just to stay asleep. That's why no one wakes up anymore; they can't handle it. I only thought to wake you because, well, you're a talking dog. I figured you'd seen some weird stuff. And I wanted to hear about it."

"I have," I said. She didn't seem shocked by me, only curious.

"My master, Merlin, he's a wizard," I said. "And this Asteria is magic. It lets me talk."

"Hmm. Makes as much sense as anything else," Winnie answered.

"Lady Nivian gave it to me. She's a Fae like Queen Mab, but a good one. She got hurt . . . so bad that she died. That's why we want to find the Grail of Waters. Merlin says it's in Camelot."

Winnie's face lit up. "Really? This is Camelot. Our farm is part of the outer ring."

"My master said the Grail was in the castle. And it pulled all of you into the Otherworld."

"The Otherworld," Winnie echoed me. "So that *is* where we are. When did your master say it happened? When did he say we came here?"

"Ten years, I think."

"I knew it!" Winnie balled her hand into a fist. "Look at this." She pulled several jars up from under her bed. I saw that they were filled with little white and yellow shards. They smelled like feet.

"What are these?" I asked, sniffing them.

"Toenail clippings!" Winnie said madly. "Look at them. Look at all the jars. I have so many."

She did. There were at least fifteen jars of toenails when she was done. It seemed odd to save them.

"I remember my twelfth birthday. We had a picnic under a blue sky. We ate roast chicken, and my brother Robb was saying goodbye to us. I haven't had a birthday since, and I haven't seen my brother. I look in the glass and I don't change—I haven't grown an inch. It's been ten years?"

Winnie was becoming hysterical. I wanted to comfort her, and I remembered something Merlin had said.

"There might be a way to bring you home," I said, wagging my tail. "Merlin said the Grail is what brought you here and what keeps Camelot in the Otherworld. My pack is trying to retrieve it for Lady Nivian. If the Grail leaves

Camelot, Merlin said the castle and everyone around it will return home. I don't really understand it, but Merlin is smart and he's often been right before."

"Really? Often?" Winnie asked, calming a little.

"Is often good enough?"

Winnie nodded. "Often is better than never. Where is your pack?"

"I don't know. The dreams in the forest led us away from each other. But Queen Mab found them."

"Do you think she brought them here to be dreamers like she did with you?"

"If she did, then I'm going to have to go find them."

Winnie leaned in close. "And *I'm* going to have to help you."

PART IV

10

❧

The Crazy Land of Camelot

WE SET OUT EARLY IN THE MORNING, BEFORE WINNIE'S PARENTS woke. She packed a sack of food and we crept out the door. I could hear Walder and Alma snoring in their beds.

The hot Fae sun was streaming over the horizon. The sky *was* different here. The clouds swirled through the air like silt in a fast-moving river.

"Eeeek!" Something shrieked. I turned and saw a monster rearing above Winnie. Its horns and claws cut into the sky. My tail dipped, but I ran to her. The creature's horned skin cast rippled shadows, and its long teeth jutted up over its lips.

"Easy, boy!" Winnie said, grabbing the monster by the neck. It calmed, and I remembered my dream from the day before. Winnie had been riding this thing.

"Good boy, Jax! Good." Winnie patted his muzzle and turned to me. "I thought he'd woken from the dream state, for a minute. You don't want to wake these things."

"What is it?" I asked, taking a step back.

"Well, what does he look like?"

I thought of pictures Morgana had shown me in a book about the Fae world. The beast had scaly skin, horns, sharp teeth, and thin, diamond-shaped eyes. "He looks like a dragon," I answered.

"Then that must be what he is." Winnie pulled herself up by a strip of leather and mounted him. "Jax didn't come with a scroll telling me about him. We were all calling him a horse, back when I was in the dream state. But he's some kind of dragonling." She reached across his neck and tugged on his horns. Jax blew gentle steam from his snout. It looked like he liked her.

"Why aren't you scared of him?" I asked. "His teeth are sharp."

"He's as asleep as my mom and dad. If you treat him like a horse, he'll act like one. Just don't wake him up."

"I won't." I didn't want Winnie to know that the dragonling scared me. His face looked like Oberon's worm sprites once they'd grown big. "Hello, Jax."

"He doesn't talk," Winnie said from above. "But he knows commands. Jax, up!" Winnie jerked on the reins.

The dragonling stood on his hind legs and snapped his jaws. His talons were six inches long, and he swiped them in the air.

"Some dragons are smarter than others," Winnie said, turning him toward the dirt road.

"I'll remember that," I said, trotting alongside but keeping a safe distance from his claws.

It was a struggle to keep up with Jax. His legs were even longer than those of the dire wolves, so though he was only walking, I had to run.

"Look at all the wheat," Winnie said mistily. "Every field is full to bursting."

The farms did look good. The grass was tall and thick. Each stalk bent under a heavy clump of grain, and they made soft, wet sounds as they rubbed together in the wind.

"It was never this good in the old days." Winnie looked down at me from on top of Jax. "The last year was the worst. A blight hit almost every field in Camelot. The plants died in a single day. No one had food or coin to buy it. And the king was too busy to notice. Father said we had to sell our horse, but none of the farmers needed a horse. All their crops were dead too."

"So what did you do?"

Winnie winced. "Father sent Robb away. He gave him the horse and told him to sell it in the south."

"Robb's your brother?"

"Yes, Robb left and then all this happened." Winnie set her hand on the dragonling's head.

"Camelot disappeared into the Otherworld."

"And Robb was left behind. He was my little brother. Only ten. I wonder if he's still alive." Winnie sighed. "I said I should go because I was bigger. But Dad said since I was a girl, 'Robb has to do it.'"

"It's not fair when someone says you can't," I said, thinking of Merlin's refusing me magic. "It makes you feel bad."

"It does, Nosewise; you're right," Winnie agreed sadly. "You talk like I imagine a dog might."

"That's because I am a dog," I said.

Winnie laughed. "That is why." She clucked her tongue. "I never thought I'd see anything new again. When the sky changed, we found ourselves among dragons, fauns, and faeries. The monsters my parents had told me about in bedtime stories were all around me. It was frightening, but not for long. A calm descended that made everything seem normal. That must have been Mab entrancing us for the first time. I don't remember how long I slept, but when I first woke up, I thought nothing would ever surprise me. But you have, Nosewise."

"I'm surprised all the time," I said. "This place is weird!"

Winnie laughed. "It is, but some things about Camelot haven't changed. The farmsteads are lonely and far apart. If Mab put your friends on another farm, it'll take us forever to find them. We have to hope she dropped them in the city, where most of the people live. Have you ever seen a city, Nosewise?"

"I've seen a few," I answered. "They've got big buildings, and bricks on the roads, and lots of people."

"Camelot's got all that, but . . . there's more to it. You'll see."

As we got closer to town, we met others traveling down the road. We approached the rear of an enormous cart piled high with grain. Mixed in with the barley and wheat, I noticed the scent of rot and flame.

"There's something wrong with that grain," I said. "Something's burning it."

She flicked Jax's reins and he picked up speed. Winnie drew up along the cart bed and lifted a sack of grain. Ashy creatures leapt up from under the sack and sparked in the air. They danced about her head and dove back into the cart. I'd never seen anything like them before.

"What are you doing back there?" an angry voice called out. Winnie kicked Jax and strode alongside the driver. I caught up and saw an old man holding the reins of two large monsters. They had tall, scaly legs, and powerful bodies covered in fur and feathers. One turned and snapped at Jax. It had a face like an eagle but the tongue of a slithery snake.

"You've got fire pixies in your grain. Can't you smell it?" Winnie shouted.

"What? Oh, curse it! Stop! Stop!" The driver pulled the reins, and his monsters slowed to a stop. He crawled over the back of his cart and swatted at the fire pixies. Winnie patted Jax and we kept moving down the road.

"What were those things?" I asked.

"The fire pixies in the grain or the griffins pulling the cart?"

"They're both scary-looking," I said.

"Nothing will hurt you here. Not while they're in Mab's trance. The monsters are a part of us now. Some are pests, like the pixies, and some help, like Jax here."

"I don't like monsters." I was thinking of the worm sprites. "They're mean."

"Some people don't like dogs," Winnie said thoughtfully. "A dog bit me once, when I was little. But that doesn't mean all dogs are bad."

"Well," I said, looking up at Jax with his sharp horns and scary teeth, "I guess Jax isn't too mean."

"No, he isn't." Winnie patted his neck. "Now look, we're coming into town."

The dirt road ahead became paved stone. A wooden sign hung from a post, but I couldn't read it.

"What's it say?" I asked Winnie.

"It says, 'Welcome to the city of Camelot, seat of King Uther and Queen Igraine . . . ' and on and on, a bunch of rules no one follows anymore."

"The king and queen live here?"

"If you can call it living," Winnie said scornfully. "My family used to come to town a lot. We loved festivals and market days and holidays when the king and queen made speeches and hosted musicians. Queen Mab stopped that when she put us all to sleep. Now one day's the same as the next."

The sound of ringing metal turned my attention to a large open shed. Within, a burly man was hammering a hot horseshoe on an anvil. When he was satisfied, he used

his tongs to lower the horseshoe to the ground. There sat a lizard as big as me, which opened its long flat beak and belched a jet of fire. Then the man returned his horseshoe to the anvil and hammered it again. "What is that?" I asked.

"A fire salamander," Winnie said. "I told you, they fit right in. All the guilds and workshops have them." She gestured to the long, low-slung buildings lining the street. Their chimneys coughed black smoke, and people and monsters traveled in and out with a lazy sense of purpose. Most of the buildings had signs I couldn't read, but there were carvings and pictures, too. One was a wheel and hammer, another a single candle, and I saw many more: gold rings, heads of cabbage, fish, and even needles and thread.

"They can make things while they're dreaming?" I asked Winnie.

She laughed. "If you'd ever had a job, you'd know work can be boring. You get distracted and your mind wanders. So Mab has them think of work and nothing else, and the city makes more goods than ever. But we've no neighbors to sell to, so the metalsmiths and weavers and wheelwrights destroy what they've made and start all over again! It's madness!"

"Why does she have them work if she doesn't want what they make?"

"I can answer some questions, Nosewise. But I don't know the mind of the Fae queen."

We kept walking through the town, peeking in windows

and keeping our eyes out for any signs of my pack. A street vendor was slicing roasted hunks of cow thigh and selling them to passersby. While he was collecting the coins from a young couple, a gang of tiny, smoking frog creatures appeared from the grass and swarmed the cow leg. The vendor shouted and swatted at them and they went sparking away.

We passed by an alley, and I saw some well-fed street dogs feasting on a garbage pile. They kept their distance from a fire salamander that ate alongside them, but not as much distance as I would have kept.

At a crowded intersection, we spotted a regiment of soldiers. They looked like Lord Destrian's men with their leather armor and serious faces, but instead of swords at their belts, each wore a long, limp reed.

"The soldiers are armed with willow branches," Winnie said. "An invention of Queen Mab's. Most likely to minimize the carnage if they wake up."

"When people wake up, it's bad?" I asked.

"It's chaos," Winnie answered solemnly. "But look where we are. This square connects roads all through the city. That way's the best well water," she said, pointing down one street. "Most of the merchants live this way"—she pointed in another direction—"and you follow that one to the biggest market, and beyond that are all the best taverns. Most townspeople cross this square at least once a day. You're a dog. Can't you sniff your pack out?"

My ears perked at the question. I took a lot of pride in my tracking abilities, but everything in the Fae world smelled rather strange. I'd learned how to correct for it, but it took a lot of concentration, and I wasn't sure I could handle picking three smells from a mess of hundreds!

But I walked into the intersection anyway.

People cursed, but they didn't run over me. A woman riding one dragonling and holding the reins of another told me to "get out of the street!" but she directed her monsters around me.

A circle of citizens, carts, and monsters swirled around me, stirring up a vortex of air. Motes of dust, debris, and hair from all over the square was sucked into the slow and lazy current. My nose was wet and twitching as I huffed huge bundles of odors in every sniff. My Mind's Nose registered each of the dozens of smells I received at once, discarding them when they weren't Arthur, Morgana, or Merlin.

I licked my nose to wipe clear the dust and dampen the crust growing on the tip. I had to close my eyes, and I felt my ears deafen as the rest of my consciousness faded away. I was only two enormous nostrils filtering the air. For a moment, I lost myself in the heart of Camelot. I knew the dragonlings, humans, horses, pigs, dogs, and griffins that made the city their home. It smelled of hot iron, dirty wool, lambskin, cooking vegetables, dead rats, and straw beds. The scents saturated my entire mind, and I finally happened upon a Certainty: My *friends are near.*

I discarded the old cookware, freshly laundered socks, house cats, garbage pails, and firewood. All I knew was a young boy with sweaty skin and dirty hair.

I chased the scent trail, and Winnie urged Jax on behind me.

"I've found Arthur!"

We shot down two busy blocks and ducked into an alley to come upon an open, grassy field. Three boys were laughing and setting up a triangle of wooden pins. A fourth boy stood with his back to me and held a wooden ball. "Watch it, boys, or my pins'll get ya!" he cried, and chucked it down the grassy way toward the pins. It rolled past them all without hitting one.

"Good job, Arthur!" I shouted. "You managed to dodge them!" I ran out of the alley and leapt against Arthur's hip, spinning him toward me. "I found you!"

"You found me? Yes, you did!" Arthur answered enthusiastically.

"You know me, don't you?" His eyes were glassy, and he seemed only half there.

"Yeah, you're a dog that I know. . . ." He squinted. "Noseguys!"

"That's close! Winnie, he knows me!"

Winnie emerged from the alley on top of Jax. "He's supposed to knock the pins down. He's bad at it." Winnie dismounted and waved her hand in front of Arthur's face. He smiled and winced when she snapped her fingers. "You're familiar to him. But he's deep in the dream state."

"Then we need to wake him up." I dropped into my Mind's Nose and I sensed the storm the two of us had nearly drowned in.

Crack! A rope of lightning and a thunderclap arced above my Asteria. Arthur watched it, delighted. "Wow! You're like a special rain man!"

"He is *deep* in the dream state," Winnie said.

"How do we scare him awake?"

"This one looks like trouble. We'd have better luck if we got him somewhere quieter."

"Merlin knew how to get rid of the dreams. He did it with a dispel. Morgana knew too. But no one ever taught me. Maybe with Excalibur . . ." I turned to Arthur and looked for the sword. "Where's Excalibur?"

"Excalibur, that's my pet pig," Arthur answered. "He's at home with the others."

"What?" I shouted. "What did you do with the sword?"

"Excalibur?" Winnie asked, surprised. "The Sword in the Stone?"

"Yes, yes, I pulled it out," I said hurriedly. "That's partly how I met Lady Nivian."

"You pulled the sword of kings? A dog?" Winnie touched her face. "I'm not in the dream state, am I?"

"Believe me, I did! I pulled the sword and had Arthur keep it for me. But he's lost it! What happened?"

"Excalibur's my sword-sheep . . . ," Arthur said, trying to put it together. "I told you, he lives at home."

"You gave Excalibur to this one?" Winnie asked, incredulous.

"He's smarter than this, normally," I said. "Queen Mab must have taken it from him!"

"All right, look," Winnie said. "We don't need him awake right now. Let's find your wizard or the girl and they can dispel him. He's impressionable now. Arthur!" she said, clapping her hands. "You follow Nosewise and me. That's what you do!"

"Yes, that's my job!" Arthur said with enthusiasm.

He *was* impressionable.

"And you call me Mistress Winnie."

"Yes, of course, my mistress." Arthur spoke in hushed tones and took a deep bow.

"Wow, he's really in a trance," I murmured.

"Let's hope your other friends aren't in so deep. Or this is all for nothing. Now get that nose working."

11

That's My Girl?

WE TRACKED BUSY STREETS AND DIRTY BACK ALLEYS. AFTER
trawling a mile of dusty bricks, I found the scent of Morgana's thick hair in front of a tannery. The strong smells of
drying leather almost overwhelmed hers. But it was enough.

We walked a way down the road and the scent grew
more concentrated. Winnie restrained Jax to follow at my
snuffling pace, and people and carts cursed as they made
their way around us.

"We're in the middle of the street," Arthur said, trying
to be helpful. "We should stick to the side."

"We walk where we walk," Winnie said forcefully. She
was unkind to the sleepers; perhaps she was mad at them
for being asleep.

"Yes, we walk where we walk," Arthur answered, almost
mindlessly.

"She came down this way," I said, leading Winnie and

Arthur around a cobblestone corner. Jax clumsily knocked over a man carrying a basket of onions.

"Hey!" he shouted. "Look what your mount did!"

Winnie pulled up the reins on Jax and turned to him. "That's just your luck today. Now gather your onions. Don't speak to us!"

The man looked surprised and then nodded meekly. He went to work picking up the onions.

"Nosewise, go on; he's in the dream," Winnie said. Her mouth was a hard line, but her eyes were wet. "That man was my uncle once. Hardly anymore."

Winnie shook her head and pointed. I put my nose to the paving stones. I couldn't imagine living here ten years, my whole life going by in a trance. I kept sniffing. My eyes blurred, and the world quieted as my nose dragged me forward. The scent of Morgana's hair and skin was as clear to me as if I were beside her.

Thump! My snout hit a heavy oak door and I was knocked back. I raised my paw to my nose and swiped. *Stupid door!*

The door was arched at the top, with a bronze placard nailed onto the boards.

"She's here," I said in a sore-nosed voice. "What is it?"

"A weaver house," Winnie said, sliding off Jax. "Queen Mab has her working the threads. Is she a smart girl? This is skilled work."

"Morgana is a good study; she knows about magic."

"It's not magic she has her doing." Winnie put two hands on the heavy door and pushed it open.

Behind lay a good-sized workshop with four long tables. Twenty women were gathered there, each with a small wooden loom. The looms were set with bolts of fabric, and each weaver had her own strand of silk rising above them.

I looked up and saw that twenty fat, slimy sacks of silk were stuck to the ceiling above the women. But the sacks had little arms with sharp claws. And they had teeth, with wet mouths that opened and closed as the women drew the silk from them.

They were monsters on the ceiling, spinning thread like enormous silkworms.

"Dragon spawn," Winnie said in a low voice. "Don't know who had the idea at first. But it's like this all over Camelot."

It was a horrifying sight. The weaver women sat directly beneath the perched monsters. They pulled their threads and weaved on their looms as though there were nothing amiss. I shivered at the crackles and smacks of the dragon spawn's mouthparts. Gobs of their spit dripped down on the women's heads, unnoticed. They just kept weaving.

"Morgana!" I spotted her and turned to Arthur. "You stay here." He nodded blankly, and I rushed to Morgana. She was seated in the last row. Her hair was wet and matted

with dragon-spawn saliva. But her fingers wove the silk between the threads.

I pushed through a small forest of legs and leapt up beside her. "Morgana, wake up!" I licked her ear. I could taste
the bitter spittle.

"Hello," she answered. Morgana's eyes were vague, but

they found me. She looked half-asleep, but I sensed a tremor inside her, as though she was trapped within herself.

"Do you remember me?" I asked.

Her eyes crossed briefly, and she nodded. "Nosewise, you're my dog."

"I am, and you're my girl. You don't belong here."

"I do belong. I'm a weaver," she said, stroking my head and returning to her loom. "Sit with me, boy, while I work."

I nudged her neck, but she ignored me. She wrapped another length of silk around the loom.

"All right! Move!" Winnie cried, pushing her way around the women. "Wake up, girl!" She clapped her hands, and Morgana regarded her for a moment. Winnie grabbed her chin and inspected her eyes. "She's deep in the dream state."

"She recognizes me," I said hopefully.

"But she's solid in the dream. It's day; we're in a crowded place. Too hard to scare her awake." Winnie put her hand on Morgana's arm. "Look, girl, now you follow us. Get up— we're leaving."

"I'm working," she said, annoyed. "You can go."

"And she's stubborn." Winnie pulled her hands to her chest. "We should try the wizard. We'll come back for this one."

"No, I'm not leaving her. Morgana is my girl, and she needs my help."

"What can you do for her now. She's lost."

"Sometimes, when I'm in a scary dream, I want to wake up but I can't. Soldiers chase Merlin in my dreams. Nivian burns and Morgana runs away. Still I can't wake up. But if someone dies in the dream, I do wake. It's too much to sleep through."

I settled in close to Morgana's face. She yanked her silken thread, and her hair swayed against my nose. It was good to take in her scent. I felt shame that in my dream at the farmhouse, I'd forgotten all about her.

"You are working in a weaving shop," I whispered in her ear. Morgana's hands flitted around the loom, and she nodded. "You're here because you ran away from your old life. Once, you lived in a house with a dog named Nosewise and a wizard called Merlin."

Morgana knitted her eyebrows.

"Do you remember why you ran away?" Morgana's hands slowed down. "You joined with a Fae named Oberon. He said he was your father. You hadn't known a father, and you believed him. He said he needed help from Merlin. Do you remember how you helped him?"

Morgana pushed on the loom. She pulled it back and pushed it away again. Her pupils twitched from side to side.

Winnie gestured for me to keep going.

"Y-you opened the Wall of Trees." My chest grew tight. With everyone dreaming around me, stories seemed to have more power here, and I found myself deep inside the tale I was telling. "The Fae man came with soldiers. He kidnapped Merlin and set your house on fire. They snatched you. Don't you remember asking them to go back for Nosewise? Your dog was in that house. You heard him bark and whine while he *burned*."

The loom cracked in Morgana's hands. She gasped for air. "Nosewise!" Her face shivered hot sweat, and I licked her neck.

"Nosewise, oh, Nosewise!" She sobbed into my mane and squeezed me tight. I licked her ear and squirmed against her. "I had the most awful dream," she managed through shudders. "I dreamed that you . . ."

Morgana pulled away and caught sight of the room. Her eyes and mouth grew wide, and she looked up.

Then she screamed.

Winnie yanked her off the bench, dragging her out from between the weavers. Morgana was in blind terror. She panicked and thrashed her arms, knocking the other weavers off their benches and into their looms. The women righted themselves and returned to their work without any expression.

I pushed through thick feet and came out from under the tables as Winnie pulled Morgana free. She led her into a corner of the shop, where a loose door partially enclosed a side room. She swung the door open and thrust Morgana inside. Arthur was at the front of the shop, happily wrapping himself in bolts of silk, when Winnie commanded him, "Follow!"

I came in on Arthur's heels and Winnie closed the door behind us. We were in a windowless room, lit only by holes in the roof.

"Where are we, Nosewise?" Morgana crouched before me.

"We're together," I said. "The three of us."

Morgana looked at Arthur. "Three? Where's Merlin?"

"We have to find him. The dreams led us apart in the forest."

"The dreams, yes." Morgana touched her temples. "And then the Fae woman . . ."

"Queen Mab brought us to Camelot. She had us walking in dreams. I thought I was someone else."

"I was a weaving girl," Morgana said meekly.

"But you're not. You're *my* girl." I pressed down my ears.

"Nosewise, of course." She stroked my cheeks and kissed me.

"I woke you, but not Arthur." I looked at my boy, who was making hand shadows in the shafts of light. "He's been harder to crack."

"Do you have a spell for dreams?" Winnie asked.

"Who are *you*?"

"That's Winnie," I answered. "She woke me up." Winnie

nodded. I put my paw on Morgana's knee. "Could you dispel Arthur's dream? The way that Merlin did?"

"A dispel?" Morgana said. "I could try it. If I could use your Asteria."

"Here," I said, offering the stone on my neck. She untangled the collar from my mane, and I felt the loss instantly. My tongue felt thick, and my lips loose.

I whined to urge her on, speechless, and Morgana let the Asteria stone hang from her hands. Winnie guided Arthur to the back of the creaky door. Arthur smiled and stood proudly where she'd placed him.

Morgana closed her eyes and spread her fingers wide. Arthur oohed at the glowing stone she held between them. Her nose crinkled and her brow slanted, and a lightning wind burst from the Asteria and knocked Arthur into the door.

"Oh, I hope that was all right. My cast is a bit cruder than Merlin's," Morgana said, shaking.

Arthur gasped and pressed his fingers to his face. "Whoa—wh-what?"

"You're in Camelot!" Winnie said, stepping in front of us. "You've just been woken by your friends. You're safe now."

"No! What?" Arthur turned in a panic.

Arthur! It's me! I tried to shout, but Morgana had my Asteria, so I was only barking at him. He spooked and grabbed the door behind him and flung it open.

The women at their worktables were all looking up and flailing with fear. Snarls sounded from above, and I crept out between Arthur's legs to see twenty dragon spawn growling and struggling to break their bonds with the ceiling.

"The waking spell!" Winnie said, peeking past the door. "It hit all of them!"

Several dragon spawn detached and crashed down on the tables. They hissed and bared their teeth. Women screamed and batted them away with the shattered looms. They fell backward over their benches, the dragon spawn wiggling in pursuit, and rushed for the exits.

"Oh, we've got to go! We've got to go!" Winnie was shouting in the chaos. "Mab will be coming now! She's going to put everyone back to sleep!"

I barked and looked to the door at the rear of the shop. Winnie nodded and grabbed hold of Arthur and Morgana, dragging them behind her. I followed in the rear. A weaver woman kicked me in the face by accident, and I smacked into the leg of a table. A dragon spawn slid off the edge and landed between me and my pack. It opened its jaws, and I scrambled backward, but the way was blocked by a broken bench. The dragon spawn wriggled closer, working its ugly jaws.

A blast of shock sent it rolling away from me and into a bale of fabric. I crawled from underneath and heard Morgana call my name. The Asteria was glowing hot, and she shot two more bursts of wind over my head. I turned to see more dragon spawn rolling away.

We charged out the back door and watched the weaving women run madly down the streets of Camelot. They screamed at every dragon they saw; some pulled their hair and fainted, while others lashed at the monsters, ineffectually batting at their snouts. But the people and dragonlings that had been outside the shop hadn't been affected by Morgana's spell, and they stayed asleep.

The wind behind us shifted, and I began to feel a gentle tugging at my mind. I turned toward the sensation. I saw a distant figure flying toward us, just above the rooftops of the town.

I barked and Winnie cried, "Mab!" She pushed Arthur's and Morgana's heads down and hurried them along the street. After shortcuts and side streets, Winnie led us into a sparsely filled tavern. The sounds from outside were dulled by its thick walls, and humans and dragonlings alike sat peaceably around the tables. The chaos of Morgana's dispel hadn't reached this place.

Winnie led us to a table in the corner and did her best to explain everything to Arthur. He'd woken up under bad circumstances and was shaking.

Morgana had plenty of questions too, and she was glad to have Winnie there to answer them. I couldn't speak myself, because Morgana still had my Asteria.

"Nosewise, I'm sorry." She slipped the woven collar around my neck. I felt my lips tighten and my tongue come back to me.

"Arthur, do you know where Merlin is?" I had to stretch my neck to see him over the table.

"Nosewise, I can just barely grasp where *I* am. So, no."

"You don't remember seeing him in your dream walks?" Winnie asked.

"Uh . . ." Arthur struggled to recall. "I lived in a dormitory of boys. Two old women took care of us, never got their names. Most days we played tenpins and wheel and stick."

"You never saw Merlin?"

"My eyes were on the pins. All I did was play . . ."

"And I was stuck weaving in a workhouse," Morgana said, her eyes widening. "But we *did* see Merlin. Yes, I remember! He came to inspect the workshop with King Uther and Queen Igraine!"

"Was he awake?" Winnie stood up from the table. I barked and wagged my tail.

"No, we didn't recognize each other at the time. But I'm sure of it now—I saw him!"

"If he was with the king and queen, then Mab's got him back in his old job as the royal advisor," Winnie said.

"Where can we find him?" I asked her.

"He's where the king and queen always are," Winnie said. "Holding court at Castle Camelot."

12

❧✖❧

The Court of Fools

CASTLE CAMELOT WAS UNLIKE LORD DESTRIAN'S CASTLE, OR the Winter's Crystal. It was set in the center of the city, so hundreds of people were nearby, but they all stayed far from the walls. "There used to be a moat around the castle," Winnie said. "But the moat didn't cross into the Otherworld with everything else. Still, people stay away from where the moat used to be." There was a thick ring of grass around the castle where nothing was built and no one set foot.

"And they use a drawbridge," Morgana observed. A large opening in the wall was set with heavy chains connected to a thick wooden bridge that lay across the grass. As we crossed, I noticed places where water had warped the wood, but there was no water here.

"What business do you have in Camelot?" asked a soldier posted at the gate. He lightly touched the dry end of his reed in case we intended trouble.

Winnie stepped in front of Arthur and Morgana. "Is the king holding court today?"

The soldier nodded. He was dressed in dirty leather armor and wore a blue cloak. At the other side of the gate another soldier idly jiggled his reed. Neither seemed particularly interested in guard duty.

"The king is in court. You may proceed." The soldier clumsily stepped aside for us.

Camelot and its yard came into full view. The castle was wide as a small valley and taller than the tallest tree. Big, square stones rose in every direction and framed ornate windows were set with oiled wood and brass. Tall parapets led to high balconies and heavy tiled roofs. The lower half of the castle was cracked with age, but the higher stories were made of gleaming black stone.

The inner courtyard was in tumult. Blacksmiths banged hammers, and sulfur filled my nose. Soldiers armed with soft reeds fenced against each other with steely resolve.

"They look like fools," Arthur said.

Dogs barked in a nearby kennel, and maidens walked arm in arm through gardens tended by rough men. Some boys were leading a line of horses into a stable, and great black plumes of smoke poured from a brick oven tended by cooks.

"Are they all asleep?" I asked Winnie.

"Each in their own way. Doing their day-to-day tasks." She turned to me and scrunched her nose. "Nothing ever changes."

We entered the castle amid a crowd of humans and dragonlings. Some smelled fresh from the baths and others like they had spent all morning in pigpens. They ambled through the great hall, paying no attention to the bright tapestries and plush carpets.

"Camelot is open to her people," Winnie informed us. "The king has always served as a judge. People can ask him for things or to settle disputes for them."

"And he helps them?" Arthur asked. I wondered if Oberon had ever played the judge at his castle when he was pretending to be Lord Destrian.

"He does all he can. Or, at least, he did before." Winnie gestured for us to gather near her, and she led us across the entrance hall. "A neighbor once got it in his head that one of my family's fields really belonged to him. He ripped out our cabbage and replanted with carrots. Father took the matter to the king and he sorted everything."

"So he was a good king," Morgana said. "Merlin always said so."

"I loved him," Winnie answered. "People still petition the king out of habit, but they have nothing to complain about. They hardly care about anything. So they just speak nonsense."

The throne room's high ceiling boasted hundreds of windows, through which the strange sunlight of the Other-world streamed. Crowds of people were packed in wooden balconies on either side of the enormous hall, and dragon-kind big and small were mixed among them. The dragons were too big for the benches and stretched over several rows, but the dreaming people of the court paid no mind.

A line of about ten people stretched down the hall to two tall thrones. A man was seated on the large throne, and a woman sat on a smaller one beside him. "The king and queen," Winnie whispered. To the king's right I saw a man in long robes, with a bushy beard and unruly hair hidden under a pointed hat.

"It's Merlin," I said, and Morgana held my mane.

"We should make way," she whispered. Several people were queuing up behind us, thinking we were in line to see the king. Winnie opened the gate of the nearest balcony, and we followed her inside. My eyes stayed on Merlin. He was sleeping, I knew, but I wanted to run to him and lick his face. Would he recognize me?

"Merlin worked wonders as our court wizard," Winnie said as she led us through the crowd of sleepers. "Everyone loved him. But when the queen became ill, King Uther ordered Merlin out of the kingdom. How could he send away a healer when his wife was sick? Then the curse came, just days later."

"Merlin once told me Camelot was his greatest regret," Morgana said. "But he'd say nothing more. In Chester, before Merlin found me, I heard people say he was the reason Camelot disappeared. I think that's why he hid in the woods."

"I heard the same," Arthur said solemnly.

It was strange to think of Merlin's life before I knew him. It hurt to think I wasn't always his dog.

"We need to get Merlin's attention," I said. "We need to rescue him."

"Speak quietly," Winnie answered. "Mab could be among the crowd. She's a face changer, you know."

I hadn't known that. I glanced around the enormous throne room. There were a thousand odors and a hundred faces. Mab's scent was as varied and changing as the stories on her dream cloak. She could be hiding in plain sight.

We reached the front of the balcony, and Merlin was only a few steps away from us. His face was kindly and his eyebrows danced as he considered the woman petitioning before the king.

"My tender-pocket beans came in full and healthy. They taste a bit like snap peas, I think. I boil them in a broth of onion and garlic." She prattled on.

"What is she saying?" Morgana whispered to Winnie.

"Nonsense." Winnie pushed back a skinny man who was crowding her. "They're all in the dream state, so what troubles do they have? But by habit we petition the king on court days. So they spout nonsense. Look, he listens!"

For the first time, I took notice of the king. He smelled of middle age and rich foods, but still healthy and strong. His beard was dark and thick, and his pupils were slightly crossed brown pools, dilated so wide there was hardly any white in his eyes. Yet he nodded in a daze as the young woman described the process of shucking a snow pea from its shell. He was asleep, like everyone else.

"Merlin!" Morgana loudly whispered over the wooden bannister. "Merlin, look here! It's me, Morgana!" Merlin squinted as though he didn't recognize her.

"Do the spell on him," Arthur said. "Wake him like you did me."

"And half the court with him?" Winnie said, knocking Morgana's hand away from my collar. "If you can't control it, Mab will come and put us all to sleep! We need to get him separate."

"Pardon me, do I know you?" Merlin had stepped away from the king and approached the balcony. The petitioner prattled on and the king took no notice of Merlin leaving, but the queen leaned forward in her throne and looked at us. Her light-colored eyes were lively and awake, which shocked me. "What's the fuss?" Merlin said. "The king is holding court."

I put my front paws up on the balcony. "Don't you know us, Merlin?"

"Why yes, I know you," Merlin answered. "Nosewise, Arthur, Morgana, and . . . Winnie, I think. Farmer Walder's daughter. I know you all."

"Then you're awake!" I said, pressing up on the rails and wagging my tail. "Quick, come away with us before Mab sees!"

"Come away with you, no! I know you as subjects to the crown, not lords who would command me away from my king. You vex me. There is business at hand. Now respect it." He was asleep.

"Nivian is dead, you know!" I shouted as he turned from us and Queen Igraine leaned forward to peek at me. "You saw her broken body in the cave. Her cheeks were clouded ice, and her mouth was cracked from nose to chin. She's dead. You said so yourself. She's your teacher and she saved us. She needs us and you're asleep!"

"Nosewise, someone will hear you!" Winnie chastised me.

Merlin stood still, but his hand was shaking. He shuddered and gasped. He crouched and turned back to me, his fingers clasping at the wooden rails. His eyes were moving rapidly, darting from side to side just as Morgana's had before she'd woken. "N-N-N-Nivian . . ."

"Nivian is dead," I repeated, coaxing him to wake. His eyebrows were dancing and his brow filled with sweat. But then something changed. It felt like a wet, heavy blanket

had descended on the room. Heavy darkness pressed my eyelids and urged me to sleep.

Mab is here, I thought.

Merlin's face went slack. His eyes crossed and lost focus. He was in the dream state again. Behind me, the children were clutching their skulls and grimacing. Morgana's eyes darted back and forth in her sockets, and Arthur tipped over the railing to the tiled floor. Winnie tried to push her way through the crowd but fell. *We never should have come here*, I thought. We'd walked right into a trap.

"Why do you come to the king's hall and speak treason?" Merlin grasped my snout in his hands. "Why did you come?"

"Because . . ." I struggled to answer, but my mind was a fog. The marble floor spun beneath my feet. Merlin's voice droned and my ears buzzed. The room went dark. I'd meant something to him once, but I couldn't think of what. There was something we needed to find. But I was tired . . . so sleepy. And I slipped away into the darkness of a dream.

PART V

13

❧

Playthings

THE PLUSH FAMILY ROOM WAS AWASH IN FIRELIGHT, AND KING Uther crawled on his knees over the carpeting. "Open the gate by king's command!" he said in a jolly voice. I padded behind him and looked over the heavy fur cloak covering his shoulders. The children were at play in their mock castle. The king had a small wooden toy full of teeth marks. I must have chewed on it.

Arthur and Morgana smiled deviously. They were encircled by wooden walls carved and painted to look like Camelot in miniature. They had toy figures too, and they perched them on the parapets.

"The prince and princess are cross with you!" Morgana said, tapping her toy. "You are not permitted within!"

"Stay out of our castle!" Arthur said, brandishing his.

The walls came up to their elbows, and there was a small drawbridge they'd lifted. This was the game they loved to play. I'd watched them at it countless times.

"Unacceptable!" The king harrumphed and shook his whiskered face. He lowered his toy and pretended to cry. The children laughed. "If you won't grant me entrance . . . I'll have to fight!" The king raised his figure and clacked it against Morgana's.

"No fair!" Arthur shouted, pushing the king's hand away. "You can't fly in the game!"

"I only jumped!" the king said, smiling.

"Can't jump either, Father!" Arthur said.

My ears pointed. Queen Igraine sat in a cushioned chair by the fire. She nibbled on a boiled egg and smiled. The room was suffused with the scents of rich food.

"Maybe magic comes into play." I heard Merlin and turned to see him at a corner table, looking up from a book.

"Yes, magic! That's just what I need!" the king said, giddily. "Court wizard! Open this gate!"

"No!" Arthur and Morgana both cried. They held their toy figures in the air, and I could see they were shaped like a boy and a girl.

Merlin laughed and closed his dusty book. He raised his staff and shouted, "For my king!" and flicked a bead of magic that tripped the latch on the castle gate. It fell to the rug with a muted thump.

Something wasn't making sense. This scene was familiar and yet it wasn't. I tried to ask a question, but I only barked.

"Good, Nosewise! Do you want to play?" Arthur asked.

"Help us guard the castle from Father," Morgana said.

"Don't joke," Uther said. "Nosewise is on my side!"

"No fair!" they shouted in unison.

King Uther was Morgana and Arthur's father, of course. I already knew that. But hadn't I heard this story before? And differently. There was a man with horns that grew out of his head. And a fight about a stone on a chain just like . . .

Morgana was wearing my seaweed woven collar around her wrist. My Asteria hung from her hand. How long had I been asleep? I ran to the toy Camelot and leapt up on the wall. "Nosewise!" Morgana laughed, as I tugged the seaweed collar off her wrist and flung it around my neck. My Asteria dropped in place below my throat and I felt my voice return to me.

"How long have we been asleep? What has she done with Winnie?"

"Nosewise, we woke up hours ago!" Arthur said, happy and dull.

"You're the one who looks sleepy to me," Morgana said. But her lids were heavy and her pupils slightly crossed.

"Queen Mab took her!" I whipped around on King Uther. "This is your fault! You sold Mab your kingdom for the Grail."

"Sold my kingdom? No," Uther answered me. "The

Grail saved my queen's life, but my kingdom is all around me. You're a part of it, Nosewise. You're our pet."

"I'm no dog of yours!" I said. "I'm Merlin's. And Morgana's, Arthur's, and Nivian's. Not yours and not Queen Mab's!"

"You're the family dog," Morgana said. "You belong to all of us."

I barked a small shock of magic and broke apart the wooden castle. "Wake up!" I shouted. "We can't get stuck here again!"

"You're frightening the children," Queen Igraine said from her chair. I whipped around to face her. She was a young woman with an oval face, and her eyes looked sharper than her husband's.

"You're the one the Grail was for. It saved your life, and I'm glad about that; I want it to save my friend. But as long as it stays in this castle, everyone in Camelot is cursed to sleep. Tell me where the Grail is!"

"A place you cannot enter," the queen said. "Guarded and apart. It is not for you." Her mouth hardened, and I felt a pressure on my mind, like a sudden urge to sleep. I fought it.

"Where is the Grail?" I barked.

"Don't talk to Mother that way," Morgana chided me.

"Very bad dog!" Arthur said, and I turned. The bad master had called me bad dog. He'd hit me too, and looked at me with angry eyes. Just like Arthur was now. I looked to

Merlin. He sat in the corner of the room, staring at an enormous, dusty book. But was he even reading it?

"Don't call me bad dog!" I said. Morgana looked at me blankly. "How could you fall for this? Oberon tried the same thing. Queen Mab is tricking you!"

"Oberon?" Morgana asked.

"The one from the stories?" Arthur said.

"The Fae!" I shouted. "Queen Mab's nephew! She's doing the same as he did. She knows you're orphans. She knows your weaknesses."

"We're not orphans," Arthur sputtered, laughing as though this were the funniest thing he'd ever heard. "I'm the prince!"

"Our mother is the queen." Morgana gestured to Igraine. "And our father is king. Nosewise, you've been part of this family for years."

"I'm a dog who talks! Isn't that strange!" I said, turning to the king. "Don't you have anything to say about that?"

King Uther squinted and fluttered his eyes. "It's not . . . strange to me," he said, more to himself than to me.

"Don't bother the king with such questions," Merlin said, looking up from his book. "He knows why—it's . . ." Merlin's eyes rolled back. "It's from my magic."

"That isn't why!" I said. "It's my Asteria, don't you remember? Nivian gave it to me and now she's dead. This is all a dream! Queen Mab wants you to forget!" I turned to

Igraine. "Don't you remember your life? You were dying and the king made a deal with a demon!"

The queen covered her mouth, rose from her chair, and ran out of the family quarters, her silken robe streaming.

"Darling, where are you going?" Uther called after her.

"Oh, she'll be fine," Merlin sighed, returning to his book.

"No, she won't!" I said. "She's trapped like all of us! Wake up!"

"We are awake," Morgana said. "Now you've made our mother cry."

"She's not your mother," I argued. But they wouldn't listen. Mab's sleeping spell was strong. "I'm going to have to dispel you now. Stay still."

"You can't cast a dispel," Merlin murmured.

"You don't know enough of our minds. You're more likely to hurt us than help," Morgana added. She stared at me with saucer eyes. Morgana was speaking, but I could tell that Queen Mab supplied the words.

I found my Certainty. *Morgana is my true friend.* She'd told me that to dispel an illusion, one had to see what was true and cast all else away. I had to know her mind, a young girl's mind. I thought on it and summoned her smells: her hair, her skin, the clothes she wore. Morgana was a thinker and a learner. I imagined the world as she must sense it from her nose.

Morgana's strengths are her passions. I know how it feels to learn something new.

But her weaknesses were harder to grasp. *Morgana mourns for parents. She and Arthur both.* I had no idea what it meant to want parents. Morgana wished for a father she'd never met and a mother she could barely remember. When the bad master had run my mother off, I'd been sad, but it was Merlin who had raised me. Morgana and Arthur were my family. Not some old male dog with white hair who I'd never given a thought to.

How can I dispel her when I don't know her pain? I might as well . . . sleep. Dreams are better than a world of pain.

"Mab!" I shouted, and opened my eyes. Her voice was in my head and, more than that, in my ears.

I spun and saw her stride through the door, her robes flailing. She smiled at me and showed bright teeth. Her cloak expanded over the entire room and played false scenes from false lives. "Look!" I shouted. "Merlin, help me!" But he was transfixed by the stories on the robes. The embroidery showed Arthur very young, a toddling boy taking his first steps while Igraine held his hand. Young Morgana, missing several teeth, sat reading at King Uther's side. Merlin was in the stitches as well, leaning down to help Morgana with her words. Arthur trained with wooden swords to be a knight, and Igraine and Uther beamed. Morgana played the hoop game in the palace yard, broke vases and pleaded for for-giveness; a thousand family dinners were stitched across the cloak's magical weaves. Uther, Igraine, Arthur, and Morgana were seated at a table with Merlin beside them. And one more sat below.

It was me, begging for scraps and wagging my tail. "I made this sweet dream for you, Nosewise," Mab intoned through heavy lips. Her eyes glowed bright, and she slid through the air toward me. Her hanging cloak fluttered over Arthur and Morgana, and they shuddered with the false memories.

"I'm going to wake them all. We're going to take the Grail and go."

"You cannot dispel them, Nosewise. You do not know their minds. You're only a dog."

"If I can't, I can't." I tried to push past her, but instead I walked right through. There was nothing to her at all, I realized; she was only dreams. "I'm still going to wake them," I said, and I barked in Morgana's ear. "Oberon killed Merlin. Nosewise died in the fire when Oberon burned down the house in the woods. It's your fault that we're dead. He tricked you."

Morgana's eyes fluttered, and she whimpered. But Mab shot her a look and Morgana was docile again.

Queen Mab laughed. "Do you think your stories are better than mine? The greatest poet couldn't tell a tale to top my dreams. You're only a slobbering dog!"

"It worked before," I said. "Wake up!"

"You woke her while I was away and before I knew what a bother you'd be. I know them better now. She wants a mother and father," Mab said, pointing at Morgana. "He wants to be safe," she said, indicating Arthur. "And the old man wants his conscience clear so he can forget he let the kingdom fall into the Fae realm." Merlin wore a drowsy smile.

"You don't know them like I do," I growled.

"Then dispel them. Work your magic. Outdeceive me." Mab twirled and opened her arms to the room. Visions spun from her robes and made my pack laugh with joy and quake with fear.

"I . . . Morgana, please, wake up."

"Don't blame yourself," Mab said, touching down to the floor. "Dogs will never know what a dream is to human folk. Men live their lives in fantasy. They obsess on their future and lose themselves in the past. Rarely do they live in the moment as dogs do."

"I dream," I said.

"Of chasing rats and running from shadows. Your very simpleness confounds me. It's why I can't keep you from waking up. But all mortal life is a shadow of Fae. All their poets, songsmiths, and painters are my puppets. I am their inspiration. Every boy or girl with a wish or a dream is en- thralled to me."

"I'm not," I said bitterly.

"I never thought a dog would catch my attention. You're more like the dragons, a beast of flesh and vital instinct."

"How do you make them sleep?" I asked. "If they don't dream like people do?"

"The mortal dreams are my power: I take their dreams, bend and work them, and weave them through the dragons' minds. It's why I brought these mortals here, so I could expand my dreaming throughout all the world."

"Why are you telling me this?" I asked. If there was one thing I was certain of, it was that Mab was a liar.

"I want you to trust me," she said, and I laughed.

"I thought you were a better liar than that."

"I speak true," Mab said, lowering herself until her eyes were level with mine. "I was wrong to dismiss the mind of a dog. There is strength in your clarity." Her ghostly hands stroked my brow. The tips of her fingers passed through my head and dipped visions of flowers and fountains into my mind.

"A dog, I've found, is governed simply by fear and love," Mab said. With my eyes I could see her hand passing through my skull, but with my Mind's Eye and Nose and Ears, there was more. "I caught you with fear," she said. I saw myself alone in the forest of dreams, Merlin, Arthur, and Morgana running away from me. "You needed your pack and I gave you one." Winnie appeared in my mind. I smelled the kitchen of Walder and Alma's house. "But you were easily woken by that girl. Who is safe, I assure you. Winnie is under my spell again and back with her family. You see, fear is no match for love. You would die to save your pack, I know. If I can't frighten you, can I make you love me?"

"Never," I said, pulling away. I watched her fingers slip out of my skull, and the visions disappeared. "You imprisoned my family."

"I've given them what they want!" Mab said, flashing bright. "*Exactly* what they want. And I can make them love you like you've never known!"

Merlin, Arthur, and Morgana surrounded me. They reached out and patted me gently. Morgana rubbed her thumbs in my ears the way I always liked. And Merlin sang tunefully, "Good dog. Good dog. Nosewise is my good dog!" He offered a generous handful of treats from the table.

My tail wagged, and their kisses made me dizzy. A *dog's dream*, I thought. *This is what I want.*

"No!" I shouted, jumping back. "I won't let you control them."

"I'll use them any way I like," Mab said. "I am the queen of dreams, but I *can* make nightmares."

"Bad dog! Down!" Merlin commanded, and raised his staff to hit me. He swung and I ducked. A shadow crossed his face, and the bad master appeared.

"Street dog! Vile thing!" Arthur grabbed a carving knife from the table and slashed at me. I scrambled and barked.

"A dog! I'm afraid of dogs!" Morgana shrieked. She hid behind Merlin's robes. "Protect me from it!"

My heart sank. My belly was lead and my legs were jelly. Merlin raised his glowing Asteria. "Begone, foul creature! Out of our sight!" Magical flames arced hot above my head. I yipped and turned tail, crying.

Queen Mab called out after me, "Dreams or nightmares, Nosewise? Dreams or nightmares?"

14

The Dragon Wall

THE ASH-BLACK STONES OF CAMELOT SWOOSHED PAST ME IN A haze. I was running the halls at full speed. Every wooden doorway I passed sprung open, and human dreamers ambled out, holding candlesticks and table legs. They swung their weapons at me and shouted nonsensical threats. "We'll clobber your toes to the ceiling!" "Get back in the barn, Sally Jean!"

Mab had them mad with fever dreams. They tried to chase me, but they were slow and stumbled down the black-brick hallways. They tripped over carpets and bumped into the colorful tapestries that lined the walls, knocking them off their hooks and sending them billowing to the floor.

So many human dreamers clogged the hallways, I feared I would crash into one or they'd catch me on the floor. As I ran past them, the castle halls branched into multiple passageways. I took quick sniffs of the floor and followed the routes that had the fewest human smells. Mab had every mortal in this castle under her control. I had to get away from them.

I ran and ran until I stumbled into a dark part of the castle where no torches were lit. The floor was free of human scent. No one had been by for a long time. No one human, anyway. I could stop and catch my breath. Mab had control of my entire pack. She wanted control of me. Could she really make them hurt me?

I sat down in the dark and focused my mind on my Certainty. *Merlin is a very good master.* It still worked, even though he'd just threatened to kill me. It was Mab's fault, I knew. It hadn't been him at all.

My Asteria glowed bright and illuminated a great pile of crushed black bricks. The walls and floor of Camelot were cracked and broken all around me. I jumped to my feet, afraid the castle was collapsing. But the stones were still. This destruction had happened long ago. Behind the ruined bricks, clean white stones reflected my Asteria light. I set a cautious paw on the debris, careful not to cut my pads on the shards of stone. A wall of glittering limestone appeared before me, with a dragon's head carved into the rocks. The white stones were cracked and scratched as though they'd collided with the broken black bricks of Camelot and won. I looked around the destroyed hallway where I was standing and wondered what had happened. Camelot had been transported to this spot in the Otherworld by the power of the Grail. Maybe this white limestone wall was something that had been here before. Another, older castle inside Camelot.

One of the white limestone bricks had shattered in the collision. I padded up to it, and as I drew near, a faint music resonated from the stone. Harp strings vibrated through the cracks. The music made the hairs on my neck stand up and my Asteria glow brighter.

I barked a spell of shock, and the white stone broke and fell away, revealing a cavernous hall that echoed with music. I poked my head through the hole, and my Asteria lit a silver-and-gold-tiled floor below me. It was too far down to jump, but a broken statue leaned against the wall. It was a stone dragon, and I hopped down its rough neck to the shining floor.

What is this place? I thought as music rang against the stones.

Here is where you'll find the Grail, a voice said inside me. But I feared what I might find with it. The dragon statue stared down at me. Its legs were broken, and a long crack ran up its belly, but its teeth were fierce. I turned from it. Sometimes courage is ignoring your fear.

This hidden castle was immense, high ceilinged and finely carved. Dragons were everywhere, some etched into the stone walls and some carved into statues that soared above me. There were other carvings too: disembodied eyes, hands, and wings. There may have been words as well, but for all the magic the Asteria had given me, I still couldn't read them.

This new hall was wide and slightly curved. I followed the bend of the wall I'd broken and saw another wall opposite it. The inside wall held a pair of double doors. Each door was as tall as three men. The right one hung inward just a few inches, and a hot breeze of sulfur and acid streamed through the crack. Something slow and rhythmic sounded within. Wind in a wet cavern? Or the breathing of a giant?

I slipped my snout into the crack between the panels. The acrid scent inflamed my nose and I pushed. The old door groaned, and my Asteria lit the dust and steam that swirled through the air. A thin fog obscured my vision, and the great hall before me was a hazy blur. The tiles beneath my feet sloped downward, and I followed them down an aisle between ancient stone blocks arching out in rows on either side of me. My Asteria light bounced through the thick air and lent a glow to the outlines of dark shapes below me.

The hall was descending into a pit, and an enormous black hill rose in the center. As I approached, my light reflected off shiny skins and wet oozes piling up before me. My nose was overwhelmed by the towering might of rot and ferment assaulting it. I smelled the decay of a hundred varieties of apple, pear, berry, and plum, both known and foreign to me. The gigantic hill of rotten fruit was so hot from composting that it bubbled and belched.

My ears flattened, and my nose burned with the sharp scents. The smell was so repellent, I could feel my mouth drying and my tongue sticking to its roof. Beyond the sounds of boiling rot I could hear the steady clatter of thuds and thwacks. There was a stream of bright-colored fruit dropping down from on high, bouncing and rolling through the gunk. I followed it upward with my eye and saw that the waterfall of fresh fruit had a source in the tall, shiny wall at the back of the pit.

An alcove had been carved in the polished rock and an odd wicker basket placed inside. The basket was shaped like a horn and full to overflowing with fruit. Plump, fleshy pears, apples, and berries swelled from its wicker form and filled the granite alcove. The excess dropped into a large wooden chest that hung from a nail directly below, but it had long since been filled, so instead of catching the excess fruit, it only provided a surface for fruit to bounce against before tumbling to the rotting mass beneath.

Another sound caught my attention. There was someone playing strings. The notes they plucked were low and quiet, the way Nivian sang to us at night when she bade us go to sleep. Was it Mab's music trying to drowse me?

But I didn't feel Mab near, and I looked for the source of the sounds. The music echoed against the walls and the hundreds of stone benches set in concentric arches behind me. The air was hazed with mist, but I spotted a second alcove carved some feet from the first. This one held a lute, which glowed a dim gold and played itself with invisible hands. The moment I looked at it, the song grew louder, as if it knew that I was listening.

"Who's playing that?" I said. "Am I alone in here? Who's with me?"

My words bounced off the walls and benches, coming back one hundred times. I spooked and sprinted partway up the hill of rotten apples and berries. The top layer was covered in fresher fruit that hadn't yet gone to goo, and I could stand on the still-firm skins and fibers. But with every step I took, my feet sank, and sweet, rotten slime rose to touch my toes.

I climbed higher and spotted a glimmer on the wall. I brightened my Asteria, and a third alcove appeared. A wide gold cup with a silver stem rested on the white limestone. "The Grail!" I ran up the rotten mountain, gasping and stirring up layers of rot beneath my feet. I'd nearly climbed half the hill when the sloppy skins and hardened seed cores beneath me rumbled. Great geysers of rotten gas burst all around me. The hot air splashed colored sap on my fur and made me gag. I tried to press on, but a geyser before me shot up a column of flame.

What is this? I thought, and turned to run, but two great

eyes blinked acid juice down scaly cheeks. I was being lifted in the air. Horns streamed steaming nectars, and I felt wet, scaly flesh below my feet. I leapt away, then fell with a splash in a slush of fruit skins. My front paws scrabbled at a solid block of pulp, but I sank into the fermented juice. My Asteria light dipped below the water, and everything went dim.

I paddled and thrashed until I hit an island of hard pulp and fiber and lifted myself onto it. Overripe strawberries and cherries that were newly fallen squished beneath my ribs, and I heaved.

A dragon rested its snout on a fruit-buried claw before me. Its eyes were yellow gold and cast a light all their own. They considered me with sleepy curiosity. Bloated, scaly skin covered its face and was pierced by pitted horns at its cheeks and the top of its skull.

This was no dragonling like I'd seen with Winnie and the sleeping folk. It was a full-grown nightmare as big as the worm sprites the day they'd attacked Oberon and Lady Nivian. It lay in the lake of rotten fruit like one of the big ships docked at Laketown.

Lady Nivian and Laketown, I remembered. I was far from home, but I'd come here for a reason. I glanced at the alcove above and at the golden Grail. Blue beams of light danced on the ceiling above the cup. It was filled with the water of life, Merlin had said.

"Do you come to offer praise and accept the gifts?" The

dragon's deep voice sent ripples through the lakes of juice. A thin stream of plump berries spilled down on his head. They bounced through a maze of horns and scales and scattered.

The dragon considered me with sleepy eyes and waited for an answer. His jaws were as long as a man laying down. Steam and sparks rose from his nostrils. "Will you offer praise and accept the gifts?" he repeated.

"Praise? Um, yes . . . good job," I said. I tried to wag my tail, but it was heavy with slop. "And the gifts . . . what are the gifts?"

"Lute of Harmony offers song," the great dragon said with tired obedience. "Horn of Plenty offers sustenance. Grail of Waters offers life."

"The—the—" My whiskers twitched and I struggled with words. The dragon was as big as a ship and could burn me with one breath. But he sank in his slop and spoke like he was talking in his sleep. "I . . . I'll take the Grail," I said, spitting out the words. Could this really be so easy?

Hmmfth. Hmmfth. The great dragon's nostrils sucked in the scent of me. Sticky eyes blinked heavily, and he exhaled hot air. I had to bury my head in the mushy pulp to cool it.

"The Grail of Waters is death for mortals," the dragon answered. He opened his foul mouth to lick clots of stinking fruit flesh from his teeth. "The waters bring too much life for mortal things. Drinking will quicken you and burst your flesh. Do you wish to die in ecstasy?"

"No, thank you," I answered meekly. The dragon breathed hot again, and I pressed my snout in the juice to duck the steam. "But hasn't one mortal drunk it? The waters saved Queen Igraine's life."

"I would not let a mortal drink and die," the dragon said again. "I am Ddraig Goch. The Guardian of Gifts."

"Who are the gifts for?" I asked. The Grail was just above me. I could bark a spell of shock and ricochet it off the back of the alcove. I'd have to catch it, lest it fall into a wet pool of fruit and sink below the juice. Gold sank, I knew; I'd seen Merlin and Morgana experiment with it in the study.

Merlin and Morgana are asleep. They dreamed with Arthur and the king somewhere in the castle. I could take the Grail. But how would I wake them? I had no idea. But without the Grail this was all for nothing. We'd escape back to a world where Nivian was dead.

"The gifts are for the Fae," the great dragon said, drawing my attention to him. "The dragonkind, the giants, and the spirits of heroes that walk the undying world. The Mothers gave them to us all. The Grail gives life. The Horn sustains. And the Lute brings joy."

"Wow," I said nervously. "That was nice of them." I leaped across several blocks of solid pulp until I was just beneath the Grail. I prepared a bark to bring it down.

A claw burst up like a wall, and jets of acidic juice stung my eyes. Hard fingers curled over my back. The dragon's scales were bloated and loose, but beneath were steel-hard bones that pinned me like a vise.

"The Hall of Gifts must be respected," Ddraig Goch groaned with some alarm. "Do not approach the Grail."

"Sorry," I wheezed. He was crushing my chest.

"Waters are not for mortals. I wish not to see you die. You may have fruit. It has not been collected in some time."

"I can see that," I managed, and tried to wriggle free. The dragon loosened his grip and blinked.

"Far too long," he said. "But how? Every day they come en masse. How could so much have fallen to decay?"

"Who comes every day?"

"All of them," the dragon said, bewildered. "The dragons of the Emerald Plains. My people . . . they come. They always come here."

"It looks like you've been alone for a while."

The dragon's eyes went wide, and it seemed that he saw the immense mountain of fruit for the first time. He gasped and struggled to free himself of it, but the slop was thick and heavy. "How could there be so much?" Something in his voice reminded me of Winnie and her jars of toenails. But the comparison ended there.

"You've been sleeping," I said.

"Sleeping!" the dragon repeated. "The witch . . . yes.

The queen of dreams. She bound the Grail. Then the men came . . ."

"Nosewise?" A familiar voice rang through the hall. "What is this place?"

Queen Igraine stood at the base of the mountain of fruit. Her evening gown was stained dark blue, and her face was terrified.

She drank from the Grail, I thought. *But how? The dragon said mortals couldn't drink.*

"Igraine, go away!" I yelled down. *Why did she follow me here?*

"Nosewise, where are we?" Her mouth twitched, and tears streamed down her cheeks. "Come away with me!" she shouted. The dragon snorted hot flames, and Igraine screamed.

"I'm busy!" I yelled, and turned my sight on the Grail. A burst of shock would do it. It would bounce off the wall and I could catch it.

Grrr! Ddraig Goch roared and reared up his head. Mounds of rotten fruit flesh and hard seed pits rose with him. He raged, and the enormous mountain of fruit he was buried in heaved outward in a landslide. Waves of filth washed over the stone benches, sweeping Igraine off her feet. She yelped and I ran to her, surfing down the sludge and leaping from bench to bench.

Ddraig Goch reared up behind. I glanced back and saw

his neck slither through the air. His eyes were changed, dully glowering at me. Chains groaned, and I saw a thick web of steel links that radiated from a collar around his neck and were bolted into the wall. Ddraig Goch was a prisoner here.

My paw slipped on a slick stone, and the world spun wet and dark. My shoulder butted against a hard stone bench. The wave of fruit guts and pits slid across me and oozed up the aisle of the chamber. I blinked the juice from my eyes and saw Igraine ahead of me, face flat against the stones and burbling into a wet pile of pulp. I scrambled up and pushed her head from the wet with the bridge of my snout.

Igraine's head turned, and she opened her eyes to me. "Save me," she whispered, and coughed. Behind, I heard the dragon's roar. The Grail was at my back, but I had to get Igraine out. I wouldn't let one person die to save another. I pressed her with my nose and she rose on her hands.

"Go!" I said, glancing back at the dragon. His chains were slack and left him plenty of room to run about the chamber. His eyes were set against us, ferocious in a dreamy way. He roared and reared forward. Igraine leapt to her feet faster than I thought she could.

"Lead me!" she shouted, though the way was clear behind her. I charged toward the doors with all my might.

But my leg slipped. My paw shot out straight behind me, completely missing the floor. My body descended and my stomach slapped against the wet stones. *Oof!* My chest crunched, and all the air went out of me. My lungs spasmed and I couldn't breathe.

"Nosewise, up! It's almost on us!" Igraine's voice echoed in my ears. *This is the end of me,* I thought. *I hope Igraine will run.* My eyes dimmed and fuzzed, and for a moment Igraine's face bent and sharpened. Then it all went black.

I couldn't tell how long I was out, seconds or minutes, but when my eyesight returned, Igraine was there. "Nose-wise, up! Quickly! We have to run!"

Ddraig Goch's head slithered threateningly overhead. Fiery jets sprouted from his nostrils and he snapped, but he stayed far above us.

"Lead me away!" Igraine shrieked, grabbing my collar. "Lead me!"

"He's not attacking us," I said, still dazed from my fall.

"He is! Get us away!"

With that the dragon's mighty head dropped down like a scorpion's tail. His jaws opened wide and crushed a stone bench. Igraine screamed. We were lucky he had missed us.

We wouldn't be lucky again. The great dragon reared up for another strike.

"Run!" I shouted.

"Yes, go!"

Igraine tried to get me up. The dragon's head was already bearing down.

But something kept me on the ground. It held me fast, looking up stupidly as a colossal dragon struck from the sky. Something here didn't make sense. If he was really trying to hurt me, then why hadn't he attacked while I was passed out?

Ddraig Goch's jaws came down on another bench, this

one nearer. I ignored his bulging neck muscles as he tore at the stones, and I focused on his eyes. They were deep in dreaming.

"He won't attack us," I said.

"He will!" She tugged at my collar fiercely.

I pulled myself away. Her hands were weak, not strong like those of the other Fae I knew.

"He's under your control," I said.

"He's a dragon."

"Queen Mab has put him to sleep."

"*What?*" Igraine paled. "Queen Mab is here?"

"She is!" I said. The illusion was already falling away before my eyes. Once I saw a true part of her, I couldn't unsee it. Her eyes darkened, her brow went sharp, and her golden hair took on a fiery hue. "She's *you.*"

"*You're* dreaming," she said, but her voice had already changed in my ears. Igraine was gone and Mab remained. I'd never met Queen Igraine at all.

"You never saved her with the Grail. Mortals can't drink the Grail waters and live, the dragon said. You only lied to the king and pretended." The dragon roared above me ferociously. The sound quickened my heart, but I didn't look. "It's all been a lie."

Queen Mab sighed. "Not all a lie, sweet Nosewise. You would have been a jewel to me."

"You'd be a bad master," I said.

"Bad or good, I am master of the dragon"—she gestured

to the monster—"and I am master of your friends. Give me your love, sweet Nosewise, or I must have your life." She reached out her light blue hand to me. Her soft, thick lips curled into a cruel smile. Sweet music played from the magic lute, sounding higher and higher as she approached.

Her plump fingers reached down toward my head. Her fingertips dipped lower, down to stir my thoughts.

But I bit them.

The flesh broke under my teeth for an instant, but as quickly as I bore down, Mab made her fingers immaterial and they passed through my jaws like smoke. She drew back her hand and sneered at me. "Stupid," she said, snarling. "Too small a mind to see the truth. I wished you for my pet."

"I *have* a master," I said, then turned and ran up the soggy field of fruit flesh. Pits caught between my toes and pained me, but I flicked them behind. The Grail was perched on the edge of the alcove. I only had to bark it down.

"Stop him!" Mab commanded the dragon above me. His long chest rained down filth and his head stretched to the ceiling. I felt the flames at my left and leapt away just as a strong blast of fire boiled the fruit below me.

He'd just missed. His senses were dulled by the dream. Mab's puppets were diminished forms of themselves; I'd seen that with Merlin. The sleep stupefied the dragon somewhat and gave me more advantage than I would have had if he had been awake.

I leapt up the fruity slope, ever closer to the wall. One bark and I could knock the Grail loose; it would fall and I would fetch. The *glop!* and *rush!* of a claw emerging from water stirred behind me. The dragon readied to strike. The air around my ears grew hot.

My mind returned to Avalon. Lady Nivian's island was a land of winter.

I spun, my Asteria sparking with white and silver rays of ice. My winter's blast met the dragon's fire head on, and steam exploded in every direction. A hot cloud of vapor filled the temple chamber, but flames came through. I ducked down and buried myself in the wet pulp. The worst of the fires were dulled by my ice, but the juice was uncomfortably warm.

When the heat subsided, I thrashed my way out and ran at the wall. My advantages were not enough. The dragon's breath was hot and his body huge. I didn't have long.

The dragon's form was cast upon the thick vapor like a shadow. His snout broke through the screen of mist and shone bright with juice and flames. The great dragon slithered down on me like a snake.

I hit the wall with my shoulder and my neck wrenched up. The seat of the Grail was above me. A faint glimmer of gold from the foot of the Grail reached over the ledge and reflected fire.

I barked high. My shock wave shot up like a whip. The

spell hit the top of the alcove and bounced downward. I heard a splash and the clattering of gold against stone. Three drops of silver, sparkling water leapt out of the alcove and sailed down toward me. The base of the Grail spun on its rim and came to rest. It was just above, waiting to fall.

Crack! An explosion of sound and splashing juice diverted me. Blue-gray wood rose from the pulp in three stands. Long finger branches clawed up and fattened, then rose high on twisting trunks of hard, reedy wood. Each stand was thick as a column and grew fast and high. The dragon shrieked in distress, and I heard Mab shouting.

As the gnarled trees swelled, fat fruits bloomed on their branches, fell off, and bloomed again. A new crop came twice a second, and before I knew it the trees withered, blackened, broke, and died.

I didn't understand. I hadn't cast a spell for trees. The droplets of Grail water had fallen and then . . . they'd touched the seeds in the spoiled fruit. *Grail waters bring too much life for mortal things.* That was what the dragon had said. The temple was a sea of pits and seeds, which were mortal.

Ddraig Goch steeled himself under Mab's spell and dove for me once more. I barked my spell of shock, and the golden Grail came down for me. I jumped up against the white stone wall and caught the stem in my mouth. The Grail dumped endless waters in a wide arc around me.

Instantly, thick trees rose and reached their sharp branches to the ceiling, catching Ddraig Goch in his neck and eliciting a scream of fire. Fat fruits and thick leaves topped my trees, and they grew high, pushing him back. They reminded me of Merlin's Wall of Trees, the heavy ring of oaks he'd grown around our house in the woods to keep danger away. I could make a wall of my own.

A hard branch caught me in the belly and spun me. The water in the Grail replenished itself, and a silver spray flew far and wide. The water hit the pulp, and more trees ascended, thick and strong.

I managed to land on my feet and run. The stem of the Grail was long and easy to bite, but the cup and foot were too wide for my mouth, so I couldn't hold the Grail upright. Water splashed at my feet, and a fortress of trees shot up behind me.

I snuck around my wall of trees and ran out to the front benches of the sanctuary. The fruit pulp there was several inches thick, and trees sprung up with my every step. I turned and saw Ddraig Goch facing away from me, burning my trees with his fiery breath. But for every one he burned, three more shot up to fill the space, all powered by the amazing Grail waters. Above him the Horn of Plenty dutifully dropped more fruit onto the pile. The Harp had fallen from its alcove, but I heard it playing somewhere. Its strings thrummed and pinged under the sound of the flames.

"He's behind you!" Queen Mab shouted, spotting me through the steam. She was near the dragon's feet and pointed furiously in my direction. Ddraig Goch stopped his fires, and the trees behind him grew all the way up to the dim glass ceiling. The Grail waters were endless.

The monster lumbered toward me. I saw the great iron ring around his neck and noticed that four of the six chains binding him to the walls had broken. They jangled against his scaly arms and belly, and the two chains that remained fastened to the wall glowed hot in the fire.

If the chains won't hold him, my Wall of Trees will. I bolted down the rows of stone benches, the Grail of Life spilling magic waters all the way behind me. I could hear the thousands of pits and seeds drinking in its life and growing enormous in a wave of wood. The dragon's chains snapped, but he screamed as he fought against the forest of wood. *Stronger than steel, my magic is.*

Mab charged down on me, screeching with fury; my trees blocked her path, but she passed through them like she was only made of air. Maybe her powers were more than I knew. She grabbed at my tail, but the fur slipped through her ghostly hand and I scampered away.

I was faster than her, and my mind was free from dreams. I burst through the old oaken double doors, and Grail waters spilled on dead stones beneath my feet, growing thick carpets of mold to pad my escape.

15

Grail Quest

THE GRAIL TUGGED AT MY TEETH. I'D LEAPT UP THE BROKEN dragon statue easily and run through the hole I'd knocked in the wall. Now I shot down the winding halls of Castle Camelot, my own scent trail leading the way to the royal rooms and my pack.

But the Grail pulled backward. The tug was slight at first, but it grew and grew until it felt like a hand was on the lip of the cup, trying to wrench it free. The Grail's waters were inexhaustible and poured down around me. Molds, mosses, and mushrooms sprang up on the surrounding stones. The waters splashed my feet, and I feared what might happen to me. But it was only the fleas and yeasts in my fur that drank the water, grew fat, and died. As long as I didn't drink the water, I was safe.

The heavy cloud of rot and airborne spores made sniffing my path near impossible. But I knew the hallways by sight as well. I turned right at a unicorn tapestry, left at a painted vase, and jumped an overstuffed lounge chair. Warm fire-light danced through the frame of a door up ahead of me. That's where they were.

"Merlin!" I called out stupidly the moment I saw him. My mouth opened wide, and the stem of the Grail slipped, yanking my tooth and splashing lifewaters. The carpets swelled with mold; leafy shoots sprouted on the leg of a chair; some turkey legs on the table gave birth to a thousand white maggots. They turned to black flies and took to the air in a cloud, then buzzed their last and dropped dead on the floor.

I tried to catch it, but the Grail flew from me and crashed into a wall. It sprayed lifewaters, and green mold coated the stones and made a sort of pad. The Grail rested there, several feet up from the floor, gently rocking back and forth. It was straining toward the Hall of Gifts, but it wanted to return in a straight line, so the wall held it.

"Nosewise," Morgana said in a sleepy voice. "Where have you been? We missed you all of breakfast."

"Is that Nosewise there?" Merlin said, just now looking up from his book. "Adventuring the castle, my boy?"

"I've found the Grail of Life!" I said. "See there! We've got to get it to Nivian!"

"A funny thought," Merlin said, twisting his beard. "Bring her a cup of water. Is this Nivian really so thirsty?"

Arthur was playing with his wooden soldiers and bent over laughing.

"Morgana, you know what to do," I said. "You know what's right."

"Of course I do," Morgana answered. "Give you a bath. You're filthy!"

They are useless. Mab's dreams had made them dull and slow, but I couldn't leave them. I had to get them out *with* the Grail.

"Sorry, pup, but have you seen Her Grace? She ran out some time ago, and I haven't heard from her." King Uther was lying on the floor and holding his prodigious belly.

"Your wife is *dead!*" I said angrily. "Mab tricked you. You bound your kingdom to the Grail, and it pulled everything into the Otherworld. Your wife is a dream that Mab created. The real Igraine is dead!"

King Uther gaped at me. His face paled, and he croaked, "Is that true?"

"I'm sorry, but yes. It is."

"No!" The king clutched his face and his lips quivered. "How could I be so wrong?"

He was easy to convince. Winnie said some dreamers were more suggestible than others. Arthur had gone our way when Morgana wouldn't.

"Order them to follow me," I said to the king. "Order them to follow me wherever I go!" He nodded and sputtered.

"By royal decree, you must follow Nosewise! Your king

commands it!" The king looked at me sheepishly to see if he'd done all right. He'd cursed his entire kingdom, but a part of me felt sorry for him. I wondered how far *I* would go to save the ones I loved. Well, I'd soon find out.

"You heard your king," I barked. "Let's move!"

It felt strange to be the one giving the commands. Dogs are much more accustomed to listening. But it was strangely satisfying to see Arthur drop his toys and do what I asked without complaining. Morgana and Merlin fell into line, but their blank faces unsettled me. I depended on their power and wisdom, but they couldn't help me.

I took the stem of the Grail in my teeth, wishing I could either hold it upright or trust one of my pack to hold it. But I couldn't walk with my head turned sideways, and none of my companions were in their right minds. We'd traveled, fought, and been captured and mesmerized for the sacred object I held between my teeth. And I didn't know how we'd get it out of Camelot, across the forest of dreams and past the Winter court, and return to Lady Nivian.

But escaping Camelot came first.

"'Ow, 'ollow me!" I said around the golden stem. Grail waters spilled behind me and turned the carpets to mold and foamy yeast.

I could hear my pack mates' feet squishing in the wet, ruined carpets and found my tail wagging. So far, things were going well.

So far didn't last long.

We came into the loud, echoey chamber of the throne room from the king's door. Just past the seats of the king and queen were the balconies. I knew my way out of the castle from here.

But we were not alone. Humans and dragonlings alike filled the balconies. There were hundreds of them, staring as though they'd been expecting us. I urged my pack forward, but they hesitated.

"'Ollow me, 'ow!" I commanded them around the cup stem, but they wouldn't move. Merlin's face was stony, Arthur's was a blank, and Morgana even seemed to sneer at me. The balcony doors opened, and humans and dragonlings were pouring in to form a wall of men and dragons at the big arched entrance. They faced me blankly and locked their arms.

I'd been too slow. Mab was here.

She floated through the wall by the king's door, gassy as a ghost. She didn't even bother to cross in front of King Uther's throne to sit on it, she merely passed through the back and crossed her legs as she came to rest on the chair. Her colored cloak flailed wide and weaved its hundred stories. But this time, each story was of me. In one, I fell from a high castle tower. In another, a horse kicked at me, landing a metal hoof to the head. One showed a monster shaking me like a squirrel.

"'Ou 'on't s'are me!" I lied around the cup stem.

"You have been most resourceful, though I wonder how much was accident. Your wall of trees has trapped my dragon. My wall of mortals, I think, traps you."

With that, the hundreds of men, women, children, and dragonlings blocking the arch at the end of the chamber began a slow and solemn march toward me. They shortened the length of the hall with every step.

"Would you harm or kill them to escape?" Mab asked. "I know that *these mortals* will kill *you.*" She gestured to my pack. Morgana and Arthur moved to block my escape by the king's door, and Merlin stepped in front of them. His eyes were hard and angry with me. He leveled his Asteria and fired a shot of hot, bright magic.

I leapt away in time. Mab's dreams controlled Merlin, but they also slowed him. The ball of magic crashed into the marble tile and lit it up with fire. All the soggy moss the Grail had grown vaporized. Singed plant flesh filled my nose.

Merlin had meant to kill me.

He fired another shot. The wooden balcony behind me froze so cold and fast it shattered. Grail waters crystallized on the floor, and the marble tiles cracked. "Merlin, stop!" I shouted, running the other way. The court visitors and dragonlings steadily approached me. They'd gotten as far as half the length of the throne room. They blocked my path. Merlin's next burst of magic would hit me or them.

I spun and barked a hot spell of shock at Merlin's flaming torch. My wind hit the fires and spread them sideways, burning the rails on both balconies. The Grail flew from my mouth and skittered across the floor toward Queen Mab. She stood and readied herself to catch it. The heat from Merlin's spell vaporized the Grail waters, and one million motes of pollen that had been floating through the air grew into bluebells, dandelions, and pansies that instantly blackened and clogged the hall.

The sudden mass of flowers caught the Grail and slowed it. I managed a great leap by sending a spell of force behind me. My jaws clamped around the thin stem, and I tumbled to the ground at Queen Mab's feet, sloshing water and leafy rot onto the wooden dais.

"Burn him!" Mab commanded Merlin. His lids were heavy and swollen, and his pupils dimly glowed. He nodded slowly and raised his staff again. Morgana and Arthur stood beside him with vague looks of horror on their faces. I saw Merlin wince and shudder audibly. I rolled away from his attack. The tiles I'd been standing on exploded.

For Merlin, Arthur, and Morgana, this was a bad dream. Between Merlin's blasts of ice and fire, I caught glimpses of them. All three twitched and lashed out their limbs. Their eyes tried to focus on me, but they jerked back and forth rapidly, sometimes disappearing into the upper lids. Merlin was murmuring something under his breath. He shouted, "Nah! Ah! Nosewise!"

He was trying to wake up. Queen Mab was making this a nightmare, but her power to keep him sleeping was strong. She stared at him, her hands outstretched and her mouth twisted in concentration. She was struggling. Merlin's mind was strong as well. He was a wizard and a wise one.

Everything in him screamed that this was wrong. He didn't want to hurt me, but Mab kept him in the dream. Fire! Ice! Shock! The spells sailed at me from Merlin's staff and made wreckage of the throne room around me.

The Camelot courtiers were approaching me still, and only a fourth of the hall was open to me. Already I could see their hair blow back from the shock and their faces blush in the heat. I was panting hard as well, but I was the only one awake. I'd gotten an idea.

I ran across the busted floor and found a pile of heavy torn-up tile and stone. Behind the bricks and underneath the leaning tile, I opened my mouth, and the Grail flew in the direction of the Hall of Gifts. But the broken stone caught it and kept it from creeping upward.

I sped out from behind and charged Merlin. He lowered his staff to face me. His lips were quivering and his teeth were chattering. His whole body shivered and spasmed, but Mab's magic just barely kept him dreaming. In nightmares, you only ever seem to wake up at the worst part. I decided I would have to give him the worst dream of all.

Merlin issued a fire spell, and I leapt right into it. My nose flushed and burned, and I closed my eyes to the heat. I summoned a small spell of ice to encase me.

I hope this works, I thought as the world flashed white and faded to black.

I dreamed of fire and ice. Swirling flames licked up my legs and chest, then were doused by icy cool mist. Rumbles and groans echoed through the darkness, and hot flashes of lightning crossed my lids.

I felt unmoored, as if I were floating across the water in a broken ship. A girl's voice was shouting in my ear. The shrill sound was outside the dream. I was sleeping, I realized. I knew I must wake up, but my groggy lids pressed down on me.

Long black hair draped over my snout. With each struggling breath, I smelled her. A girl was on top of me, her hand holding firm on my collar.

Fire! The burning tore at my chest. I wailed, but my throat was swollen closed, so I could only squeak. The black hair parted like a curtain and revealed a white-bearded man. He brandished a stick above me. His beard shook as he shouted, "Wake!"

A golden glow lit up the black hairs near my face. My Asteria went cold and vibrated in a soothing rhythm. A small, soft hand ran up my scorched legs and chest, and the screaming pain dulled to an ache. I felt my throat open, and cool air filled my lungs.

Morgana, I smelled her. Morgana. Morgana.

"You woke us, Nosewise." Her voice rang in my ear. "You scared us awake. We saw you burn."

"Take them! Tear them apart! My grail!" a voice screeched in the distance.

An old man droned on, "Wake! Wake!" The sounds of spells and screams and shouts of horror echoed through the throne room. The black hairs waved in front of my eyes while Morgana's quick hands worked my wounds. Merlin's sandaled feet shuffled on the stones and sent dispels behind me. Mab's cloak fanned out across the hall and showed scenes of my pack as monsters. She sent her evil dreams to the hordes of mortals behind us. Merlin struggled to throw them back.

Arthur tried to tackle Mab, but he went right through her. His face hit the dirty, shattered stones.

They all woke up. They saw me burn, and it was too much to sleep through. They woke up because they love me.

Through the black curtain of hair, I saw a small, glowing hand on a cooked slab of meat. *A sausage?* I thought, looking at blackened skin. The cold sensation hit me, paw to elbow. Morgana's hand was on my leg. That sausage was me.

My snout was burned pink. My whiskers were gone, and for the first time in my life I could look down and see my chest. My mane had been reduced to a few blackened tufts.

I woke them too well, I thought, groaning. The skin on my neck cracked when I craned to see the Grail. Morgana moved her healing hand to soothe the skin, but I was more relieved to see the golden cup still against the stones where I'd set it.

Get the Grail, I tried to say, but I only wheezed. I made to stand, but my legs quivered, and Morgana pushed me to the floor.

"Wait!" she cautioned. "I'm not done."

My eyes closed at the pain, and for a moment I felt as if the whole world was rumbling.

I had not felt wrong.

Merlin was the first to shout. Then Arthur, then Morgana. I heard them one after the other. Morgana's curtain of hair was gone. Her hands left my Asteria. Without her cooling touch, my wounds burned hot. Merlin stumbled back and tripped on a broken tile. An explosion of stone and dust burst from the wall behind the thrones. A hail of pebble-sized shards rained down on us and felt like hot pokers on my flesh.

Gray shadows combined into a ceiling-high monster. Ddraig Goch stood over us, its dreaming eyes clouded and wandering.

"Dragon!" Arthur shouted, and ran straight through Queen Mab, tripping over the stones and stumbling beside me. She ignored him. Mab faced the dragon, her arms outstretched and her cloak of dreams sending misty shadows into his mind. The great dragon's eyes rolled and fell upon us. Hot steam jetted from his nostrils.

"Dispel," I whispered to Morgana. She grabbed hold of my Asteria and mumbled something I couldn't hear. Merlin was at it too. He sat on the floor in front of us, head bowed in concentration, sending wave after wave of white pulsing light at the dragon. Morgana sent hers from my Asteria in support. They bombarded Ddraig Goch with clear thoughts from clear minds.

The dragon lumbered toward us, his eyes still sleeping and his head reared back to strike. *They don't know the mind of a dragon,* I thought. *They can't. They have human minds for human dreams. They think in words and deeds they mean to do. The dragon has no ambition. He's a guardian. He watches steadfast over what he's trusted to protect.*

Just like me.

My mind went blank, empty of words. I was filled by love and duty. Obligation to my pack: Merlin, Morgana, Arthur, and Nivian. I would always keep them safe. I would always risk everything. They were my true purpose.

A great white blast of light left my chest and filled the room. Hot flames leapt from Ddraig Goch's mouth and singed the ceiling. Yellow sparks and black smoke swirled around it, and filled the hall.

When the smoke thinned, the dragon looked down on me with clear eyes, wide awake.

Queen Mab said something fierce, but I couldn't hear it under the screams of humans running from the hall.

Nearly a hundred men, women, and children were pressing through the crowd and streaming through the wide throne-room arch. Merlin had dispelled the lot of them, and without human dreamers nearby, Mab had no power to keep the dragonlings asleep.

It happened so fast that, by the time I turned back, Ddraig Goch was already upon me. Morgana leapt over my body and screamed. I knew she meant to protect me, but it hurt like fire when her elbows hit my red, bald legs. My raw skin dragged under her rough lace tunic. "I've awakened him," I gasped, shocked at how much it hurt to stand. "Dragon, take us!" My voice was a croak, but he heard me.

"Where is the Grail?" The dragon breathed hot against Morgana's neck. She cried and skittered away.

"You can have it when we're done," I said. "Take us away!"

Queen Mab's cloak had expanded over half the hall. The dragon's eyes crossed for an instant, but I straightened them. I could feel his mind somehow. Call it dog sense. I kept him on his duty. He was guardian of the Grail, just as I was guardian of my pack. Merlin cried out somewhere. Morgana I could feel shivering behind my tail, and Arthur shouted gibberish, his voice so panicked I could pick him out from the crowd. But none of them mattered right now. It was me and the dragon.

"As guardian, I cannot hold it," Ddraig Goch thundered in his smoky voice. "Take it and I will carry you away."

I was off through the noise and the smoke, limping across the shattered tiles. My toes were pink and blistered, and sharp pain shot up my legs with every step. I tripped and plummeted toward the jagged floor.

Two hands caught under my unsinged tummy. I belched and coughed, but stayed upright. "You're too hurt," Morgana said. I couldn't turn my neck to see her.

"The Grail . . ."

"I've got it!" a blur shouted as it passed me. Arthur leapt over clattering stones and grabbed the golden Grail roughly by the cup. He whipped around and thrust it in the air, splashing life-giving waters down on his skin and clothes. Instantly, blue and yellow foam bubbled up from his skin and his tunic, growing a hairy bed of moss. Arthur yelped and tried to brush the foamy slime from his skin, only to shake the Grail and spill more lifewaters. His stockings and shoes bloomed.

Merlin was beside me. A wrinkled hand of cold silver light ran down my chest and soothed my burns and swells to a dull numbness. "My boy, I'm so sorry. The dream—" I stopped him with a rough lick of my tongue. I slurped the scraggly hairs of his beard into his eye, and he half laughed.

"I had to wake you up."

"You did that, my boy." Merlin grasped my cheek. "You did indeed."

"Get on the dragon!" I shouted at Arthur. The lifewaters had run through a hundred generations of whatever tiny spores and molds lived on his skin. I had smelled Arthur, so I knew that many called him home. His clothing was a thick skin of moss and fungus that squished and bubbled.

"On the dragon, boy!" Merlin stood up, shouting. He thrust out his staff, and a golden hand of light grabbed Arthur by the waist. Ddraig Goch lowered his mighty wing, and Merlin's magic dragged Arthur onto the folds.

Mab appeared from behind the dragon's tail, and her many-visioned cloak twirled. It glowed with embroideries of Arthur throwing her the Grail. Merlin cast a spell to clear Arthur's mind, and I saw his small fingers grip the Grail tighter. "Help Nosewise to the wing!" Merlin commanded Morgana, and he rushed forward into the fight for Arthur.

My legs failed me and I fell. My eyes went dim and the world spun. Merlin had only numbed my injuries, and I'd probably done myself worse by falling. Thin arms crooked beneath my belly and I was off the ground. Morgana grunted under my weight, and my snout bounced against the tiles.

I saw blurred bricks with no idea if they were floor, wall, or ceiling. At one point I was on my back. Morgana's arms dragged me up some sharp and scaly floor to a perch high above. We came to rest, and Morgana sighed loudly. I was leaning against what must have been Ddraig Goch's enormous shoulder bone. The dragon ran, and everything rocked from side to side.

As my head lolled, Merlin stood over me, casting spells behind. Arthur was on his stomach, face toward me, the Grail pinned between his chest and the skin covering the dragon's spine. It splashed lifewaters down his clothes and bubbled up vines like an overripe potato.

Queen Mab was cursing and chasing, while her dream cloak flung out in waves, beckoning us to sleep. But my mind was filled with love for my pack. And I was wide awake.

16

⌒◌⌒

Scared of Heights

DYING WEEDS FROM ARTHUR'S CLOTHES FLEW OVER MY HEAD. But my eyes were fixed on Castle Camelot, with its towers, pavilions, and yards pulling away from me. The dragon stomped up clouds of dust, and the spilling Grail waters exploded them into flowers, grass, and fists of mushrooms.

I heard shouts and the clatter of steel. I struggled to stand, but Morgana had one arm around my stomach. So I only managed to lift my head.

"The gate! Close the gate!" shouted the soldiers on the wall, still caught in Queen Mab's dreams. Huge iron counterweights dropped, and the great gate swung up like a bear trap.

Archers drew their bowstrings. More than fifty stood along the walls, and I feared some would hit their mark. Ddraig Goch was headed straight for the gate, bringing us in close range of the arrows. I prepared a spell of shock to knock them from the sky, but the archers surrounded us in a half circle; I didn't know if I could stop them all.

Merlin held on to the dragon's scales with one hand and his staff with the other. "Take the ones on the right, I'll take the—" Merlin started, but a brass horn drowned him out.

"Loose!" all the soldiers said in unison. I panicked and blasted shock to my right. Merlin's staff wobbled, and his spell hit Ddraig Goch's head. The beast roared, and I curled into a ball.

I heard the *whfft!* of the arrows cutting the air and screamed when something poked my side. But it was only Morgana's hand gripping me. Floppy arrows dropped down from all sides. They flew a few feet and fell limply into the yard. "Nock!" the commander called again, and all the archers readied new ones. They were flexible, and instead of steel triangle points on their heads, they featured blooming puffballs. The horn sounded, and another round of arrows filled the air.

Queen Mab had armed her foot soldiers with reeds instead of swords, and just so she'd filled her archers' quivers with sunflowers. They nocked and unloaded on us again, but this time my tail was wagging. Merlin laughed. "They send good tidings!"

Ddraig Goch skipped the castle gate entirely and leapt into the air. I wished he'd warned us. He flexed his massive wings, and Merlin rolled into Morgana, who fell onto me. I flipped and tumbled down the dragon's back, past Arthur.

My paws found purchase on a rough spot, and I dug my claws into his scales.

I was dangling. Ddraig Goch ascended straight into the sky. I can't say how anyone else kept their grip, because all my energy was focused on not falling. "Stop!" I shouted. "Too steep!" but the dragon didn't hear me.

A few droplets of Grail waters came down past my head. I closed my eyes and turned away, but I felt a bead of moisture enter my left nostril. Its scent was overwhelming, and I blew out hard through my nose. If I inhaled it, I'd die.

With the drop came a jet of yellow-blue foam made of all the little things that lived inside my nose. They swelled through a thousand generations of slime. Merlin and Morgana had always said I needed to mind what I put in my nose and mouth. Now I wished I had.

The ground was far away, and we were high above it. There below us were the castle's towers and gates and the town it had taken me half a day to walk through. They looked as small as toys. Humans and dragonlings crowded the streets, but they looked no bigger than ants.

Angry ants, or frightened ones. Even from up here I could see they were swarming. An entire kingdom below me was waking to find themselves in the Otherworld, surrounded by dragons. Maybe dangling from the sky wasn't the worst place to be.

Ddraig Goch leveled off. His wings stopped beating,

and he took on a slow, graceful glide. He swooped gently through the air, and his back flattened.

I stood on unsure legs. Merlin, Arthur, and Morgana were lying down, gripping the dragon's scales. "Hey!" I called in a raspy voice. "Ddraig Goch!" I barked.

The dragon's enormous, curved ears perked, and his neck curled like a whip, swinging his face over his back. The motion made him tilt slightly, and I dropped to my forepaws to keep my balance.

"We are far above," he said in a low, droning voice. The wind was streaming past my ears, and I had to flatten them.

"Why did you climb like that?" I shouted. "We nearly flew off!"

Ddraig Goch's eyes went wide. "Mab is low. Now we are high! We still have far to go to break the bonds."

"Please be careful with us! If we fall, we die. And the Grail will fall with us."

"Help!" a high-pitched voice called out, nearly lost to the wind and sky. "I can't hold it anymore!"

I crawled down to Arthur and found that his face was buried between two bumpy scales. His right hand held on to a small round horn, and his left was wedged beneath his chest. Lifewaters spilled from under him and grew heaps of mold and weeds. I wondered if he had any clothes left under the filth.

"I can't hold this, Nosewise. It's pulling too hard."

The veins in his neck and forehead popped. His toes were jammed into a bank of scales. The Grail was lifting his chest up and away from the dragon's flesh.

"The farther we fly from the Hall of Gifts, the greater the pull will be," Ddraig Goch moaned. "But I cannot grasp it! I am forbidden!"

"Let me!" Merlin shouted, scrambling over to Arthur on hands and knees. He shot a band of golden light from his staff. The lifewaters stopped spilling, and the constantly growing mass of life died off, leaving a thick slime covering Arthur's body. Morgana crawled down the dragon's shoulder from my right and shouted something. "What?" Merlin asked. The wind was getting louder.

"There's a place by the neck. A ridged fan of horns!" Morgana shouted.

"I cannot bear the Grail!" Ddraig Goch protested.

Morgana ignored him and waved Merlin up. He magicked the Grail from the pile of slop that covered Arthur from head to toe, and Morgana took hold of the stem.

She held the Grail in a steady, upright position so the lifewaters wouldn't spill. Merlin's magic countered its pull, and Morgana guided the Grail to the horny ridge at the base of the dragon's neck.

"Mind the placement."

"I am—just keep it steady."

"That's the spot. If it's upright, we'll have less trouble."

"I have said," Ddraig Goch shouted, "I cannot bear it!" He roared a jet of flames that sent Merlin scrambling.

Morgana grabbed the stem of the Grail just as it was about to fly off into the sky. "You must!" she shouted at the dragon. "Let us break the bonds and send Camelot back! Mab is putting them to sleep again as we speak. Humans and dragons alike! Do you want that?"

She didn't wait for an answer. Morgana heaved and set the Grail in between two spiny horns in the ridge behind his neck. Ddraig Goch moaned, but he made no further complaint.

Merlin crawled to her side and set to work magicking the thing in place. They capped the waters so they would not spill, and Merlin surrounded the cup in a halo of rainbow light.

"Will it fall?" I asked, when Ddraig Goch had turned back to his path.

"If the dragon flies straight, then no. The bonds I've placed—"

"Master! It's coming loose!" Morgana said.

Merlin turned back to the Grail and reinforced his magic.

"If we get the Grail far enough away from Camelot, will it break the bonds?" I asked. "Will everything return to how it was before?"

"It should," Merlin answered uncertainly.

"And then to save Nivian," I said. "Will the dragon be strong enough to take us all the way?"

Merlin gave Morgana a worried glance. "Not all the way. We must cross through the portal in the Winter Woods ourselves. But my magic should be sufficient to carry the Grail that short distance. At least, I hope."

He looked over his shoulder at the kingdom below us. The chaotic city streets were a distant sight, the castle only a small white mound. Long square fields of grain and rows of vegetables stretched as far as I could see. Little houses and barns dotted the landscape.

I wondered if Winnie's farm was one of those specks. Mab had put her back to sleep and sent her home to her family. Maybe we'd passed already, or maybe her little house was at the other end of the farmland. All the houses looked alike from up here.

"The girl that helped you," Merlin said when he saw me peering down. "Winnie was her name?"

I must have looked worried, because Merlin cupped my head beneath the crook of his elbow and rubbed my neck. He was careful to avoid the burned places. Morgana crawled up beside and scratched my belly. Arthur was hunkered down, lower on the dragon's back, steadily scraping the muck off himself.

Morgana laughed. "Arthur! Need some water for washing? We have a cupful here!"

He was not amused.

"That's terrible," Merlin said, but laughed all the same.

"Don't you have a spell that can wash me clean?" Arthur called up the dragon's spine. "This stuff won't come off!"

"I would help you, but I'm afraid you may not have any clothes left under all that muck," Merlin called down. "I'd advise you to wait until we return to Avalon. I know it's uncomfortable."

Arthur's body made a sucking sound as he pulled away from a pile of goop. I padded down toward him and gave his face a lick. "Nosewise, that doesn't help," Arthur called, pushing me away.

"I'm trying to clean you!" I answered.

"Your tongue's just as dirty!"

"No, it isn't!"

Merlin and Morgana laughed again, but a sudden roar drowned them out. I spun and saw fire fill the air. The dragon shrieked and beat his wings against the sky.

"What's happening?" I shouted, but Ddraig Goch didn't answer. He stretched his neck and grunted flame with each exertion. The muscles tightened around his spine, and his scales flattened. I crawled my way to where Merlin and Morgana huddled by the bony ridge, weaving spells.

"Is it the Grail?" I asked, but my words were lost under the dragon's fire. The golden cup shuddered and spattered lifewaters in the air. I ducked to keep them off me and heard Arthur shout as they splashed him.

"The farms! We're coming to the end of them!" Morgana yelled.

I glanced over the dragon's shoulder and saw that she was right. The farmlands stretched before us, then ended. The billowing grain fields and farm roads gave way to giant twisted trees. Mountains rose behind with ghostly, dancing lights.

We're flying the Grail out of Camelot, I thought. *Ddraig Goch is breaking the bonds!*

More flame and heat exploded from the dragon's mouth. Each wingbeat made a small tornado. The hot air burned my lungs, and the three of us had to turn away, staring down the dragon's tail. Merlin kept his magic on the Grail, and I cast spells to cool the air.

Morgana gasped and grabbed what was left of my mane. "The castle!" was all she said, and choked on the heat.

I tried to cast another spell, but my focus was gone. Moments before, the castle of Camelot had been a speck against the blue-gray sky. Now it was gone. The town had disappeared too. The farmland below us vaporized like water. Crops and animals and outbuildings blinked out of existence, leaving only confused dragonlings in their wake.

"Camelot's gone," I said as dust and mist rose from the Otherworldly fields.

"They're going home," Merlin said.

Behind us, Ddraig Goch laughed uproariously. His shoulders lifted high with each bellow. His land was free of invaders, and I was happy for him. But all the laughing and cheering made it hard to hold on!

17

You Can Never Go Back

Dᴅʀᴀɪɢ Gᴏᴄʜ ᴀɢʀᴇᴇᴅ ᴛᴏ ꜰʟʏ ᴜꜱ ᴀʟʟ ᴛʜᴇ ᴡᴀʏ ᴛᴏ ᴛʜᴇ Wɪɴᴛᴇʀ Woods. But he took a winding and circuitous route. "Between the old seat of Camelot and the Winter Lands lies the Great Dreaming. Queen Mab's power may be lost in my land, but she will hold sway there. Millions of mortal dreams still dip up from the shadow world."

"Ours isn't a shadow world," I said.

"But it is only a shadow. There everything dies and nothing lasts," Ddraig Goch replied in his booming voice.

"Well, why do we call this the Otherworld?" I asked Merlin.

"I didn't invent the name," Merlin said. "It's what men have called the world of dreams, magic, and the soul for generations."

"We've got our world, and we just call this the 'other one'?" Morgana said unsatisfied. "There must be a better name."

"The Magic, Dreams, Dragons, and Fae People Forever world," I offered after thinking for a moment.

"Good effort," Merlin said, patting me on my head.

"The Awfulworld," Morgana said, scowling. "Everything that's ever happened here is bad. Oberon lied and tried to hold you prisoner in the Summer Lands. Lady Mithriel trapped us in the Winter court. The forest of dreams was a nightmare, and whatever that dragon place is called was filled with bloody dragons! Nothing good comes from here."

"I wouldn't speak so badly of a land when you're riding on the back of its chief guardian," Merlin said, and Morgana blushed. "Besides, the Emerald Plains were never made for us. They are for dragons. The bottom of the ocean wouldn't seem a good place for you either, but to a fish, it's perfect."

"Everyone here is evil. Everywhere we go, they try to kill or capture us," Morgana argued.

"Not Nivian," I said. "And not Annaquin! They're *good*!"

"Sure," Morgana answered. "But think of everyone else. What is wrong with this place?"

"Things have been changing in the Otherworld. I am ignorant of much of it, but I know a little," Merlin said darkly. "There was a time when Lady Mithriel loved her cousin more than anyone and never would have conspired against her. But that was long ago. The mortal plane and this Otherworld were once very connected, as I understand it. The

Fae people were respected and lorded over the houses of men. But things have changed. The two worlds grew deeper and farther apart. Magic itself has become rare in our world. Five people out of every seven don't even believe it's real; many fewer know its secrets."

Merlin peered down at the land below the dragon's belly. We were flying higher and higher over the ground, but I could see golden halls and marble stone arches, roads made of glass bricks and what looked like thousands of ghostly shapes striding down the walkways.

"Say, what is this land, Dragon?" Merlin shouted over the beating of Ddraig Goch's great wings. "I don't recognize it."

"A realm we had to pass to stay away from the Dreaming. But not one for mortal eyes to see or mortal minds to know!" Ddraig Goch roared and pressed higher into the sky, until the strange land below was only a blur.

"Were those—" Morgana began to question, but Merlin stopped her.

"Some things are better not to know," he said, looking down and then catching himself.

I wasn't sure what they were talking about, but it looked nice enough to me.

"Why is magic becoming rarer?" Morgana asked once Ddraig Goch stopped ascending and his back became level again. I looked down his spine at Arthur, who'd scraped as much gunk off himself as he could without being naked and dozed in the cradle of the dragon's shoulder bone.

"The Otherworld and our world are wrenching apart. No one knows why. Though I suspect the growing separation has something to do with why Mab was so intent on increasing her territory. Less magic comes to us as the worlds drift asunder, and fewer dreams cross over to Mab. Dreams are her only power. If the two worlds completely leave one another, her kingdom will be a beggared one. So taking over the Emerald Plains and the dragonkind may have been an attempt to make a new home for herself."

"Why didn't Lady Mithriel want us to save Nivian?" I asked, angrily. "She's her cousin, and you said she loved her."

"Well, ambition plays a part, that's for certain. With Nivian gone, Lady Mithriel becomes the queen of the Winter court, and the Winter Lands are the most prominent in all this world. The real question is, why did her people support her?"

"How could they let Nivian die? She's so good!" I shouted.

Ddraig Goch huffed. Merlin gave him a worried glance. "There was a time when Fae saw themselves as protectors of us mortals. But more and more, they want nothing to do with us."

"And why would they?" Ddraig Goch growled. Merlin's

face went flush. The dragon had heard our whole conversation. "Look what *your* dreams did to my land!"

"That wasn't our fault! Mab did it all!" I shouted.

"Bah!" Ddraig Goch belched a hot fire and turned back to flying.

"The way Nivian told it, Oberon and she were the only Fae who wanted anything to do with us mortals anymore. We've seen that ourselves with the Winter court. I can only imagine what the Fae of Summer now think of Oberon's folly. He bred sprites capable of killing Fae, all to get a sword and become a mortal king."

"Well, I don't care what they think!" I said, standing on unsure feet. "Let them all stay in their ice castles. We're bringing this grail to Nivian. And it's got nothing to do with them."

"That's what I say too," Morgana answered. "Oberon can rot. And all his Summer friends can dance to an endless bonfire in the stinking woods. Nivian is our *friend*."

Merlin chuckled. "You speak like I'm arguing for the Fae. I can't tell you how many have tried to kill me."

"What about you, Arthur?" I shouted across the dragon's back. "Where do you stand in all this?"

"Hmm?" He looked up at me, sleepy-eyed.

"He can barely stand at all," Morgana said, laughing.

"You jest, but he's lucky. If he'd swallowed any of that water . . ." Merlin shot a respectful glance at the Grail.

"Very dangerous for mortals. Be careful when you handle it. Once we cross through the portal, it will be very hard to move. I'll need help from both of you. The pull right now must be enormous."

"Merlin," Morgana said, tugging on his sleeve. "Ice mountains."

"What?" My master turned, and over the horizon appeared snowy mountains, miles high. We were back in the Winter Lands.

"The Winter Woods! They're right there!" Merlin stood as straight as he dared and called to the dragon. "The portal is not too far off, I think. In that big forested valley, some thirty degrees to the left. See it there? Halfway between us and the horizon."

Ddraig Goch groaned and lurched leftward. I could tell that the Grail was pulling hard on him, leagues and leagues from its home. The scales it pressed against were swollen, and every time the dragon beat his wings to drive himself forward, the Grail indented his flesh more and more.

"There's something in those trees," Morgana said, pointing to a forested plateau high and to the right. "Movement. Lights."

"Lights?" Merlin said, whipping his head around. Bright blue-white flashes swept up from between the trees and arced toward us. Misty streaks trailed them in the sky. They cut the air with a whooping sound.

"Attack!" Merlin shouted, and pounded the head of his staff against Ddraig Goch's neck. "Dive, Dragon! Attack!"

Blasts, crackles, and roars filled my ears, and Merlin's hand pushed my head down behind the bony ridge. Shattered ice rained down from the sky, and I slipped on the half-frozen slush flooding Ddraig Goch's scales. The dragon was roaring and tilting. My back paws went out from under me, and I slid down the scaly trench between two of his ribs and crashed into Arthur in the crook of his shoulder bone.

"The snow people!" Arthur screamed, flailing his arms and falling away from me. I bit at what I thought was his shoe to catch him, but I only caught a mouthful of sodden mush. Arthur scrambled and grabbed a protruding scale at the base of the dragon's wing.

Merlin was shouting something behind me and sending spells of fire over my head. I ducked down and crawled up the crook of the dragon's shoulder bone. Ddraig Goch's entire right wing was frozen in a solid sheath of ice. Near me the ice was thin and cracking under his strength, but down by the tip it was thick. Merlin's fire spells worked to melt it, and Ddraig Goch himself turned his head and blasted like a fiery furnace at the wing. I had to leap backward to avoid the flames, and a great boiling cloud covered everything.

I tried to find Morgana and Merlin in the fog, but all I could see were fire spells zapping through vapor. Merlin, I judged, was somewhere near the spine, but Morgana had no magic to illuminate her position. Arthur was steadily screaming his head off, so I knew he was still on the dragon.

I clambered my way across the moving scales, half-blind. The dragon was tilting wildly, right to left; he dove and tried to climb, but could only writhe in the air. I caught a hint of Morgana's sweat diffusing through the vapor and followed it, not knowing what part of Ddraig Goch I was running on.

Then I broke through the mist. At the base of the dragon's neck, I found her huddled in front of the bony spinal ridge, crouched and struggling with something. The frozen, boiling wing was behind her, and the rest of the dragon's body was veiled in steam and smoke. Morgana glanced up and caught me with her eyes, terrified.

Another salvo of bright blue-white blasts arched up from the hills, now far behind and to our right. A horde of figures was spilling out of the trees and shooting spells at us. *Lady Mithriel's forces*, I realized. They'd come to bring the dragon down and stop us from delivering the Grail to Nivian.

I barked and leapt over the bony ridge at the base of the dragon's wildly shifting neck. "Magic! I need magic!" Morgana cried. She was pressed bodily against the front of the ridge and grasping the golden stem of the Grail. She had her right foot on the base of the cup and her left hooked underneath a dragon scale. Her teeth were gritted and her face was flush. She leaned on the shaky, shivering Grail with all her weight, but it clattered and bounced, trying to jump up out of her hands.

"Magic!" she called again. Merlin's power wasn't holding it. He was fighting off the Fae attack. Ddraig Goch's wing thawed, refroze, and shattered. We were going down.

"I don't know how! I don't know how!" I shouted, and scrabbled with my paws, attempting to help her hold down the Grail. We were dropping so quickly toward the ground that the lifewaters were flowing up in a steady, skyward waterfall.

Morgana glanced behind and screamed. "Nosewise, we'll crash! I can't hold it!" My paws were slick and wet, and the cup rattled and cracked my toenails. Ddraig Goch's neck was swaying wildly, and we were rapidly approaching the tops of the trees below, not falling straight down, but gliding into them. The first branches struck the dragon's belly and burst into a thousand splintering pieces. The dragon curled his neck in front of us—I didn't know if he meant to protect us from the trunks as they exploded against his head, but we were shielded from the worst of it. Broken halves of fifty-foot trees flew over our heads like the pins in Arthur's bowling game. The dragon's body bounced and shook below us, and Morgana and I both lost our grip on the Grail.

I saw it leap up from the scaly skin, and the whole world slowed down. The golden cup glistened with lifewaters as it sparkled and flipped. Upside down, it flew higher and higher, clearing the bony ridge at the top of Ddraig Goch's spine and flying backward and away from me as quick as an arrow from a bow. Everything I'd come so far to find and fought so hard to keep was gone in a blink of an eye, and all that remained was a slow flowing arc of the sacred lifewaters, spilling up and away from me.

A sudden power surged through my legs, and my Asteria glowed bright. I pounced up and over the ridge and flew down the line of the dragon's spine. My mouth went wide, and I thickened my tongue at the back of my throat. My nostrils flared, and I felt the airborne stream of lifewaters fill my mouth with a cold, fresh explosion of chill. My jaws slammed shut and my lips tensed firm, biting down on the lifewaters and holding them in my mouth the best that I could. The dragon's body flew out from under me, slowed down by breaking tree trunks. I tumbled through the forest backward, my rear catching a felled log and spinning me against the dirt and dead branches.

I collapsed into a limp pile, but my mouth stayed closed and my tongue stayed thick. Some lifewaters dribbled from my lips and sprung new trees around me, but I swallowed none of them. Gases filled my mouth, burbling and growing. The lifewaters were going to work.

Hfffph! I blew a jet of foaming blue gunk out through my nose. I couldn't swallow, I knew, but stuff was growing inside me and I had to get it out.

Hfffph! I emptied my lungs, expelling the molds, jellies, and slimes that were burbling up between my cheeks and at the back of my throat.

Don't swallow. Don't swallow. Don't swallow, I thought.

In the wake of the broken trees in front of me, I saw Ddraig Goch trying to raise himself from the forest floor. He moaned and growled and flexed his heavy neck to slough off the smashed trunks and branches that buried him. I inhaled a quick breath of clean air and felt my mouth fill with slimy gas again.

Hfffph! I blew my nose and limped over to the dragon. He'd know what to do.

He roared and snapped at a sharp trunk that was stuck in his neck. Then he screeched and looked behind him. Merlin was there, working magic on the half-broken wing. He was leaning heavily against his staff and blowing sheets of hot air over the frozen flesh, melting it clean. The foam rose in my mouth again and I blew it out *Hfffph!* Merlin startled at the noise and ran to me. "Nosewise, help me! We need to thaw the rest of the wing. Arthur and Morgana are clearing branches from his scales; we need to get him flying again." Ddraig Goch moaned, and I saw Morgana and Arthur on the other side of his neck, wrenching a plank of wood out from between his talons. "Come! I need your spells. Fire, Nosewise!"

Hfffph! I blew foam from my nose and took in a quick breath while my throat was clear.

Merlin's face went dark. "What did you do? Spit out it, now! It will kill you!"

Hfffph! I expelled more foam from my nose.

"Spit it out!" Merlin commanded and grabbed me by the muzzle. A few drops of murky lifewaters dribbled from my lips to the forest floor. Seven thin, reedy trees sprouted up where they touched the ground and forced Merlin away from me. Mats of moss and mold spread wide under my feet. The sudden color and sound spun the dragon's head, and he fixed his large yellow eyes on me.

"The Grail has gone home. I cannot fly. And they come for you," Ddraig Goch said. My head was spinning. Explosions of bursting wood and ice rang through the forest. They came from somewhere off in the trees beyond the dragon's broken wing. They were near.

"What did you do? What did you do?" Arthur shouted when he found me. "It's poison!" He reached out his hands, but didn't dare touch my cheeks. I pulled away from him.

"You have to spit it out, Nosewise," Morgana said. "If you swallow, it will kill you."

Then I won't swallow it, I said wordlessly. I could hold it in my mouth until we reached Nivian. The trees beyond the dragon were shaking with Fae forcing their way through.

"What are they going to do to us?" Morgana asked, terrified. If I spat out the lifewaters, the Winter Fae might leave us alone. But Nivian would stay dead. It'd be the same as killing her.

"Can you fly us out?" Merlin shouted at the dragon. The great Ddraig Goch struggled under his own weight. He managed to lift his massive body with injured arms, but his wing was iced and broken. He shouted a blast of fire. "I cannot fly. You must run! They won't harm me."

"Let's go! Let's go!" Arthur shouted, tugging Merlin's arm.

"They're mounted, boy. We can't outrun them!" Merlin pushed him off. "We need to fight. Where is the sword?"

Arthur's mouth went agape. "The sword?" He patted his chest and hips. "Queen Mab took it when I fell asleep. She took it off me!"

"How will we fight them without Excalibur?" Morgana cried. Trees rattled in the distance and roots snapped as rough magic tore them up from the ground. Leaves, branches, and broken trunks were tossed above the tree line. They were nearly upon us.

I pressed between Merlin and Morgana and faced the shaking trees behind the dragon. I lifted my head, making sure to keep my mouth shut tight, and blew a bit of foam through my nose. My Asteria glowed hot. I would not lie down and surrender the Lady's life.

"It's a fight we can't win!" Merlin shouted, but I ignored him. I smelled the hot heat of flame in my Mind's Nose and huffed a long torch of fire into the rumbling trees. Ddraig Goch roared and sent an inferno of flame to join mine. Merlin cried, and fireballs flew forward into the approaching line of Winter Fae. Their shadows looked blue-black in the heat of the fires. I spotted Queen Mithriel, in silhouette, mounted on a blackened sleigh. She cried out to her soldiers, and ice and water exploded from her magic, steaming mist up through the burning trees.

The lifewaters were tingling in my mouth, and foam clogged my nose, threatening to choke me. I cleared it along with flame and heat and wind from my Asteria, but it wasn't enough. The Fae shadows were bigger and darker and approaching through the firestorm. They froze the ground, and ice shields sprung up to meet our flames. They'd break through and slap the lifewaters from my mouth, or force them down my throat to kill me. And what would they do to my pack?

The doubts seized my mind and evaporated my Certainty. The flames in my Asteria died down to sparks. "Nosewise, it's not enough. They're pushing through. Spit it out!" Merlin commanded me. He stopped his fire spells, and the Winter Fae advanced further. Ddraig Goch still spewed flames, but Merlin shouted, "Spit it out!"

I looked down at the spot on the forest floor in front of

me. If I released the lifewaters now, then Lady Nivian would stay always dead. There'd be no going back to the Hall of Gifts; Mithriel's Winterguard would never allow it. The last hope for her would end with a dribble of drool. And a few trees would sprout instead, and die a moment later.

I relaxed my lips.

"Fires in the Winter Woods!" a voice sounded. Trees broke and leaves rattled and the sounds of a dozen panting, barking wolves behind me turned my head. "Get on my sled, you fools, and fly!" Annaquin appeared behind us, riding at the rear of the dire-wolf pack. Her sled slid off the hard-packed snow down to the melted forest floor. The dire wolves howled, and Arthur cheered and jumped aboard. Morgana grabbed hold of my mane and tugged me up onto the sled. Merlin threw himself on with his staff, and Ddraig Goch shouted, "Go!" He blasted a hot jet of fire at the Winter Fae opposite the charred clearing and evaporated their freezing spells.

"Fly!" Annaquin's rough voice rose above the roaring fires, and the dire wolves lunged and huffed. The lifewaters were still safe inside my mouth. Morgana held me round the chest with one arm and clutched the rail of the sled with the other. Arthur steadied Merlin, and the world pulled away behind us—flew away, really—disappearing the Winter Fae, the burning woods, and the great dragon into a forest of racing frozen trees.

18

Breathless

SNOW JOGGED UP IN HEAVY CLUMPS FROM THE DIRE WOLVES' churning feet. The double row of wolves wove between the trees like a hairy snake with Annaquin's sled as the tail. We rode in silence. Crackling booms from ice-shattered trees rang out behind, and the Winterguard's ice bears roared through the forest.

Merlin, Morgana, and Arthur surrounded me like a shield. They held me secure in the center of the sled, and their gentle hands softened the bumps and wiggles we suffered from the ice trail. Merlin's magic rested carefully at the back of my throat. He held the lifewaters there so none would slide down from a gasp, and he reinforced my lips with his subtle power so nothing would shake loose when the trail tossed us.

The only one who spoke was Annaquin. "Gee! Haw! Mush! Slow!" She directed the pack with a deft touch. The words carried meaning for the wolves, I realized, just as my trick words had for me. *Sit! Stay! Speak!* I missed the days when those were the only words I knew and simple tricks made me happy. The Winterguard's magic echoed through the woods like thunder. Each bump threatened to knock the lifewaters out of my mouth or down my throat. This was no easy trick.

"Calm. Calm!" Merlin cooed when he felt my tongue tensing. Even with his magic touch, I found it grew harder and harder to breathe. My snout wheezed awful foams, and slimes threatened to drip down my throat.

"They're gaining," Morgana said fearfully. "Annaquin! They're drawing nearer!"

"Not far off now! Hah! Mush!" Annaquin shouted, urging on the dire wolves. The great dogs flexed their muscled haunches and kicked up mists of snow and ice. "Gee! Gee!" Annaquin cried, and the wolf pack slid through the thicket of trees to the left. The woods were so dense here that the sled skidded into tree trunks on both sides and rocked us terribly. My head was thrown back, and involuntarily I began to gulp, but Merlin's magic held my throat in a frozen state, hard and hurting.

"Sorry, boy—we're so close!" Merlin said.

"Hold on, Nosewise!" Morgana stroked my half-burned mane.

"We're here, boy. I know this place!" Arthur exclaimed. "It's where we met the wolves!"

I saw it too, the rough clearing Arthur had found when he'd gone off to mark a tree. Our tracks were still here. The snow was mashed where the dire-wolf pack had inspected us. The sled turned up the hill where the trees were burned from Merlin's spell when he'd first met Annaquin. *We're here!* I stupidly tried to say, but Merlin's magic sealed my mouth shut. He looked down at me with wide eyes.

"Keep true, keep true," he mumbled, strengthening my throat and clearing the foam from my nose with spells. "Right ahead! The great tree!"

"I see it, Man Wizard! Wolves, ho!" Annaquin cried.

Trunks were cracking a thousand feet behind us. The ice bears' growls carried across the frozen wind, and a snowy storm of magic nipped at our heels, only damped by the labyrinth of trees.

"The portal's near closed! You need to widen it!" Merlin shouted over the howling winds.

"I'll hold it open long enough!" Annaquin cried. "And I'll slam it shut behind you! Whoa, my babies! Whoa!" The pack broke their run and planted thick paws in the icy frost, spraying sheets onto the big tree with the small cavern buried inside its roots. The stout Fae woman leapt over the rail of the sled and danced on top of the snow like she was weightless. Arthur jumped out next, then Morgana, and the two of them trudged through the snow. Merlin took up my rear and kept his Asteria at the base of my neck. We rushed across the crackling ice, and I only had time to glance back at the dire-wolf pack. *Good dogs*, I thought.

"Come on, boy!" Morgana shouted from below me. She and Arthur had already slipped down into the damp hole between the great roots of the tree. I toppled into their arms, light-headed, but their quick hands and Merlin's magic kept the lifewaters safe in my mouth. It was dark in the hole, but I saw Annaquin's shadow as she ripped the tiny puckered portal beneath the tree into a wide tunnel and three pairs of hands ushered me into it.

"Go, my boy!" I heard the Fae woman say from behind. "And give the Lady my love!"

The dark spiderweb sensation shut my eyes. Winds whipped by my ears, and rough stone rose to catch my paws. My Asteria glowed, and murky shadows danced around the damp cave I found myself in. Lady Nivian's form was huge and monstrous against the rocks. Her face and hands were recognizable enough, though made of fractured crystal. She still had that enormous crack between her nose and mouth, and her eyes were cold stones.

I lowered my head and the lifewaters swirled gently in my mouth. *Hfffph!* I blew foam from my nostrils. The cave brightened, and I turned to see Merlin standing over me, his Asteria casting bright rays of light.

Dead Oberon was thrown up against the opposite wall. His flesh had broken down to rotting wood, and termites crawled over his neck. Mushrooms sprouted from his ears and armpits. His mouth was an ashy frown.

"Merlin, what should he do?" Morgana asked. She and Arthur were there, huddled together, keeping their distance from the dead Fae on either side.

"She needs to drink," Merlin said simply. "I'll help you reach her." He lowered his staff, and the light dimmed. A block of clouded ice rose from the cavern floor. Snow and water from elsewhere in the cave flowed and grew it higher. Rough steps formed up the wall of the cavern and ended with an icy ledge that jutted out below Nivian's broken face. I gave Merlin a hesitant glance, and he encouraged me. "Go to her. I'll keep you safe."

"Be careful, Nosewise!" Morgana called.

"Don't slip!" Arthur said. The children followed me up the staircase. They cradled me with their hands so I wouldn't fall. My legs were weak from all the fighting and Merlin's fire. My throat ached from the effort of clearing everything through my nose. My head was light and my vision was cloudy, but my lady needed me, and in my mouth was the only cure to save her.

I climbed the slippery steps, Morgana and Arthur bracing me from behind, Merlin minding all his magic from the floor. They supported me in every way, and I took the highest step. "Careful on the ledge," Arthur said, roughing the smooth ice with his fingernails so I wouldn't slip.

Morgana held my belly as I walked. Nivian's face was long and crumbling. The crystals that remained of her were clouded and cracked. Her dull eyes stared into the darkness.

"What does he need to do?" Morgana asked Merlin. I was reminded of the days before I could speak for myself.

"She has to drink it. But I don't know if she can."

"Nosewise, pour it between her lips," Arthur said. "But mind the crack!"

"I'm releasing the spell binding your mouth. Be careful not to swallow," Merlin reminded me.

My tail wagged to show him I understood. I crept so close that my nose touched the rough rock that was her upper lip. The Lady's mouth was as wide as my head, and I dipped down and loosened my lips. Lifewaters spilled from my mouth into hers, but they ran down the bottom of her lower lip and drained through the crack, dribbling down her chin.

"Nosewise!" Morgana called, but I saw it. I licked the waters back into her lips. I licked her again and again from the bottom of her chin to the inside of her mouth. My tongue scraped against the rough rocks she'd become, but I kept licking and licking so the lifewaters would coat the inside of her crystal mouth.

My tongue was burning, and I felt it was on the edge of splitting open, when the Lady's mouth softened. Ice and

stone cracked, and her mouth was wet and spongy and
sweet. Warm breath sighed into my snout.

I pulled my head away and shook. The Lady's lips were

flush with life. Her rocky cheeks flaked away and revealed dusty flesh. A wordless cry went up from all my companions. I turned and saw awe on their faces. A pair of enormous hands embraced me. The Lady's form broke off the wall, and the ice stairs Arthur and Morgana were standing on crumbled. But I barely noticed. The Lady's eyes were alive again, and she looked at me with love.

"Nivian!" I yelped and licked her dirty face. My tongue lashed away the dust and rubble and showed her bright blue flesh. I nuzzled her cheek.

"My lady! My lady!" the others shouted. Her warm hands rubbed my ears, and her kisses tickled my snout.

"Lady Nivian, you're alive again," I said.

"I—" The Lady gasped and seemed to choke. "I—ulp!" She looked behind me and her face went pale. She garbled something and set me down on the cavern floor.

"What are you—" I asked as the Lady floated past me, over Morgana and Arthur looking up from the ground. Merlin reached out, but she pushed his hand away. She was tall still, twelve feet high, but she floated even higher to the mangled giant against the other wall. *Oberon.* I saw her kiss him, full on the lips, giving him the last drops of the lifewaters.

Vines cracked and the sound of leaves rustling filled the chamber. Lady Nivian shrank down to her normal height and settled on the cavern floor before us. All five of us stared at the broken tree man as mushrooms shriveled, bright new wood replaced old rot, and green flesh shed its bark. An antlered man broke off the wall and fell to the floor, leaving a giant dry skin suspended above him as though he were a molting beetle.

Oberon breathed hard and steadied himself with weak hands. Merlin lowered his Asteria and I readied mine, but Lady Nivian waved us both away. Oberon's eyes blinked open and he glanced between us, his teeth shattering.

"You did it," he called out in a hoarse whisper. "You brought us back."

"We saved Nivian," Merlin growled. "She gave you the draft of life."

Oberon winced in pain, his eyes fluttering.

"Why did you save him?" I asked, shivering. Both Fae looked weak. Neither could take a fight.

"He is going," Nivian said, her voice light and raspy. Oberon looked at her and nodded.

"I give thanks with a humble bow," Oberon choked out, dropping low. "Worry not; I leave you now." With that he turned and half walked, half crawled up the twisting length of the cave. We watched him slink away into the darkness in silence. After a long time, Lady Nivian drew my head to her hip with a warm hand.

"Come, children," she said. "Let's go home." Her eyes were warm, and she embraced us all. "For you must tell me *stories.*"

Epilogue

THE NEXT FEW DAYS WERE GIVEN OVER TO REST. THE LADY WAS alive again, but weak, so she stayed close to me for protection. She called me her loyal dog, and that made my tail wag. The baby worm sprites had abandoned the island. The magic had all disappeared while the Lady was dead, so they'd gone off in search of other food.

The house in the hills was undamaged, and we rested there with the Lady. Merlin offered up the bed in his room and hunkered down on a mattress of straw in the great room alongside Arthur and Morgana. "I now see why you two complained," he said after the first night. "I'll be sure to expand the house once Nivian is well again."

I slept by the Lady's side. She did not sleep, as far as I could tell, but rested wordlessly all night and day. Sometimes she stroked my face and spoke in a language I could not understand. Words have their place, I'd learned, but sometimes they only get in the way. For now, I was the Lady's guard dog.

Soon we were all feeling better. Merlin magicked bricks in the snowless yard for a new wing to the house as Arthur futilely tried to give direction. Morgana offered to continue our magic lessons, but I told her I wanted to stay by the Lady until she fully recovered.

Some nights we spoke with only our minds, as we had when we'd first met. I told her stories of all we'd done and seen in the Otherworld: the Winter Fae, Queen Mab, the dragon. She crinkled her nose and told me tales of the Winter court. For years, she said, there had been plots against her, from some wanting power and some looking to break with the mortal world. She'd fought them all off. Once, Oberon had plied his tricks on Annaquin, her faithful servant. He wooed her and convinced her to spy on Nivian for him. She later admitted her guilt, and though Nivian forgave her, Annaquin renounced her place at court and took to the Winter Woods.

That's why she hates Oberon, I thought.

Why, indeed, the Lady said in turn. *I forgave her just as I forgave my brother. She mended her ways, though he did not. Still, it is always better to forgive. Fight if you must, but love when you can.*

One morning, we woke to Avalon covered with ice. I ran from the window to the Lady's bed and licked her face. *I'm nearly well,* she said. *Just let me rest a little more.*

We snoozed together until noontime, when I heard a shout. Merlin always left the door slightly open so I wouldn't explode it when I had to go out. In the yard I found him waving his staff as a tiny glowing blue strand chased him. Arthur grabbed one of the earthen bricks Merlin had cut and threw it at the tiny worm sprite. The creature spiraled to the ground and Morgana smashed it with a rock.

"The worm sprites are returning now that the island is strong." Nivian stood in the doorway behind me. "None of us can stay here any longer."

"My lady," Merlin said, bowing his head. "You should be in bed."

"No more time for that, my apprentice. You gave me life and another chance. Now I must make good on it." She raked her hand through the sky and the wind shifted. "I've just knocked off course a boat filled with friends. It will land in the bay by the polished boulders. Meet them there and have them take you away, before more worms arrive."

"We're not going to leave you," I said, squinting in the strong wind. "I won't let them hurt you again."

"I am going too," Nivian said, her eyes sharp and alive. "To the Otherworld, to press my claim. I cannot let chaos reign in the Winter court. I am queen."

"Lady Nivian, are you sure you're well?" Merlin protested.

"Let us protect you!" I said. "We'll come with you!"

"To the Otherworld?" Arthur said, warily.

"Nosewise, don't tell her that," Morgana whispered.

"Fear not, children," the Lady said in her soothing voice. "I owe your dog and master my life, but they owe me their allegiance. I am queen of the Winter Lands and sovereign of your magic." A twinge of emotion gripped my chest. Nothing feels better than to obey a *good* master. "Make your way to the polished rocks and take the boat off this island. Keep yourselves alive, for when I return, I will need you again. My wise . . ." She touched Merlin's arm, and kissed his cheek. "My good . . ." She took hold of Arthur's chin. "My brave . . ." She embraced Morgana and whispered something in her ear. Morgana nodded tearfully. "My faithful, loyal, honorable friends." She dropped to her knees and stroked my ears. I licked her face and she laughed beautifully, like music.

I was so happy that I hardly noticed her hands shrinking from me as the Lady dropped away into the thick, cold snow.

By the polished boulders, we did find a boat and two old friends.

"Arthur?" Guinevere called, shielding her eyes from the afternoon sun. "Nosewise! All of you! We thought you were dead! For a second time!" She jogged up the shoreline toward us, her father Leodegrance crunching through the snow behind her.

"I'll be!" he said in his booming voice. "You're all alive! Again!"

I rushed down to them and leapt on Guinevere's chest. "We saved Nivian!"

She petted my ears and kissed me. "Oh? But from what? We knew something terrible happened."

"After you left port, Guiney and I followed you in a swift boat," Leodegrance said. "All the snow was melted; the woods were torn apart and covered with these terrible worms."

"It's a long story," Arthur said. He approached Guinevere and awkwardly tried to embrace her. They ended up patting each other's arms. "Um . . . Guinevere, you—you look different."

"I think I should," she said. "You've been gone nearly a year."

"A year?"

Morgana and I looked to Merlin.

"Yes, I feared as much," Merlin said. "Time in the Otherworld doesn't work quite the same as it does here. I'm afraid to ask what we've missed. But right now, we really must return to Laketown. The island has become unsafe for us magic users."

"We'd take you, but with *this* wind . . . ," Leodegrance

said, wetting a finger and holding it up. Instantly, the powerful current changed course, blowing gently toward Laketown. "That's strange."

"Not as strange as what we've seen," Merlin answered, smiling.

"I don't want to go to Laketown," I announced. "Is it true the lake connects to rivers and streams?"

"It is true, Nosewise," Merlin said. "But why do you ask?"

"Because," I answered, looking up at the Laketowners, "I want them to take us to Camelot."

"I told you it would be here!" I shouted when we came around the river bend and the castle appeared. The journey had been long, three days by boat, traversing lakes and riding rough river currents. We told Guinevere and Leodegrance the whole story, starting with Nivian and Oberon in the cave and ending with the ride on the dragon. And then Camelot was before us, the same farms we'd seen in the Otherworld stretching over hills and vales for miles, and in the distance a thick circle of city surrounding the tall castle.

"I'll be," Leody said. "Camelot returned. What *magic*!"

"Just like the stories," Guinevere said in awe.

"The castle *is* pretty big," Arthur offered. "I could sh-show you around if you like."

After a lot of walking and sniffing we found Winnie. She was working a field off a ways from her farmhouse with a mule and backhoe. Everything was just as before, minus the strange sky and the dragonlings galloping about. I picked up my pace and barked. "Winnie!" I shouted. "It's me!"

She turned and dropped the backhoe in the dirt. "Nose-wise?" She caught me in her arms as I tackled her and licked her face and arms. "Good dog! Good dog!" After she'd greeted my pack and made acquaintance with Guinevere and Leody, she told us there was something she needed to show me. She retrieved her shovel and led the whole lot of us to an apple tree on the other side of the farm. She dug and I scratched at the ground with my paws. The soft soil gave way to a torn length of wool with something very stiff inside it. Winnie pulled the treasure from the ground and shook the dirt off.

"About a week ago, I heard the beating of leathern wings in the night and woke with a jolt. I ventured out in the dark and discovered a dragon staring at me. He was enormous, the size of a great hall, with a long, serpentine neck."

Guinevere and Leody were dumbfounded, but I knew at once. "Ddraig Goch!"

"That was the name he gave. For a moment I thought we'd gone back to the Dreaming." Winnie shook her head. "But he laid this woolen scabbard down and said that after the dragons drove Mab off, they found this in their castle. He asked me to keep it safe for you."

Arthur reached out, and Winnie offered the object to him. He removed the woolen sheath, and Excalibur glowed bright and sang like a bell. Guinevere and Leody gasped and knelt before him.

"The Sword in the Stone!" Leody shouted. "My king!"

"Papa, not this again?" Guinevere said, and lightly knocked him on the head.

"Right! Sorry," he said, getting up. "It's just so awe-inspiring, you know."

Along the way back to Winnie's farmhouse, she told us all that had happened in Camelot since its return. Most people thought their time in the Otherworld had been a dream brought on by poisoned water or spoiled grain. Some things, though, were impossible to explain away. Winnie pointed to a tall, broad-shouldered man pulling cabbages in a nearby field. He looked like a younger version of her father, Walder. But I didn't think returning to the mortal world would have affected his appearance.

"It's my little brother, Robb. When he heard Camelot had reappeared, he came home. But now he's nearly twenty! My parents can't understand it. He tells them we were disappeared. More and more outsiders are journeying here to see what happened. The truth will come out."

"Then King Uther must reassert his rule," Merlin said, concerned. "The realm is still in chaos, with warlords and petty knights carving out fiefdoms. We need a steady hand at the helm."

"Too bad the king's a fool," Morgana muttered.

"The king is gone," Winnie answered. "Packed up and left in the night. The rumor is he dressed himself as a beggar and snuck out of the castle. No one rules."

"From shame, I expect," Merlin said.

"It's all his bloody fault," Morgana complained.

"But you have the sword," Leody said, turning to Arthur and me. "The one who bears Excalibur is the rightful king."

"But can a dog really be king?" Guinevere asked. "People believed it in the tavern. But they were full of mead. Who would take him seriously?"

"Why can't a dog be king?" I asked, puffing my chest. Morgana laughed uncontrollably.

"A question for another time, I think," Merlin said, chuckling himself. "We are weary from the journey and could use some food and rest. Winnie, please, may we join you at your table?"

"Of course," she said, and led us toward her home.

"It's easy to be king," I murmured under my breath. "Simpler than saving everyone over and over."

Winnie's house was just as I remembered it. She went to the pantry and gathered an armful of bread and cheese.

"You are loyal, wise, and fair," Merlin said. "All the things a king should be, Nosewise. But the realm will not accept a dog who talks, much less one who tries to rule."

Morgana was still laughing to herself as she broke a loaf of bread. "I don't really want to be king," I said, snatching up the scraps she dropped. "I just want us to live together in peace."

Morgana rubbed my head, and Arthur sat tensely between Guinevere and Leody. "Does there even need to be a king?" Morgana asked. "Why not a queen?"

"Perhaps," Merlin said. "But someone must rule. The realm has suffered far too long from chaos."

"Before we solve that, everyone must eat," Winnie said, pouring soup into bowls from a kettle on the fire.

"Cheers to that!" Leody answered. He raised a mug of ale he'd found somewhere.

"Yes! To the wizard dog!" Guinevere shouted, banging her hand on the table. "Or the wizard's dog? Which is it again?"

"Um, it's uh—uh—" Arthur stammered, his face grown flush.

"Both!" I shouted, my tail wagging happily.

Just then, the front door swung open. "I didn't know you had guests." Winnie's father, Walder, froze when he saw me standing on the table.

"Hello," I said. "Do you remember me?"

"Oh no, I'm dreaming again!" he said, and fainted straight away.

Merlin, Morgana, and Winnie were fast at his side. Winnie shook him lightly, and Merlin murmured spells to revive him. But I wasn't worried. Dreams couldn't hurt you, I'd learned. They might be scary, but you can always wake up.

Author's Note

I've spent a lot of time considering this question: "What is the theme of *The Wizard's Dog?*"

My first book, *The Bully Book,* was about the power others have to shape your identity, and the difficulty of defining yourself.

My second book, *The Zoo at the Edge of the World,* asked what kind of relationship humans should have with animals and whether we had the right to control them.

After thinking about it for a long while, I believe I finally discovered the profound theme of this book series.

Dogs are the best.

They just are. Dogs, in my opinion, are the greatest things humans have besides each other. From the time humans began our civilizations, dogs have been by our sides as protectors, helpers, advisors, and buds.

My dog, Bowser, is one of my closest friends. He was my inspiration for Nosewise and dutifully sat by me every day of my writing, providing comfort and support. I hope that you, dear reader, have a dog like that in your life. If you don't, there are plenty of wonderful animals in shelters right now, literally this very second, waiting for their chance to have a happy home.

I'd like to thank everyone who has helped me get out the message of the beauty of dogs. That includes my excellent editor, Phoebe Yeh, and her assistant, Elizabeth Stranahan. Bob Bianchini, whose art direction of this book was awesome, and Dave Phillips for his genius-level illustrations. My agents, Doug Stewart and Dana Spector, for their advice and support. And Nick and Matt for helping me shape the story.

And Bowser, of course, for just being himself.

You can send questions and comments (or pictures of your pup!) to Eric at ekgwrites@gmail.com.

About the Author

Eric Kahn Gale's dog, Bowser, has yet to retrieve a missing magical artifact, but he's still pretty good at playing fetch. His spunky personality is also the inspiration for the lovable Nosewise, whose first adventure, *The Wizard's Dog*, was praised as "an entertaining adventure full of humor and heart" (*Booklist*) and "an ingenious . . . twist on a familiar tale" (*Kirkus Reviews*).

Eric is also the author of *The Bully Book* and *The Zoo at the Edge of the World*. He lives in Chicago with his wife and Bowser. You can find Eric on Twitter at @erickahngale, on Facebook, and on his website erickahngale.com.